MATTHE[W]

FURIOUS WAKE

A JASON WAKE NOVEL: BOOK 5

Copyright © 2022 by Matthew Rief
All rights reserved.

No part of this book may be reproduced in any form or by any electronic or mechanical means, including information storage and retrieval systems, without written permission from the author, except for the use of brief quotations in a book review.

This book is a work of fiction. Names, characters, businesses, places, events and incidents are either the products of the author's imagination or used in a fictitious manner. Any resemblance to actual persons, living or dead, or actual events is purely coincidental.

Cover Design by Stuart Bache of Books Covered
Line and Copy Editing by Sarah Flores of Write Down the Line, LLC
Interior Design & Typesetting by Colleen Sheehan of Ampersand Bookery
Proofreading by Donna Rich, and Nancy Brown of Redline Proofreading

ALSO BY MATTHEW RIEF

FLORIDA KEYS ADVENTURE SERIES:
FEATURING LOGAN DODGE

Gold in the Keys
Hunted in the Keys
Revenge in the Keys
Betrayed in the Keys
Redemption in the Keys
Corruption in the Keys
Predator in the Keys
Legend in the Keys

Abducted in the Keys
Showdown in the Keys
Avenged in the Keys
Broken in the Keys
Payback in the Keys
Condemned in the Keys
Voyage in the Keys
Guardian in the Keys

JASON WAKE NOVELS

Caribbean Wake
Surging Wake
Relentless Wake

Turbulent Wake
Furious Wake
Perilous Wake

Join the Adventure!
Sign up for my newsletter to receive updates on upcoming books on my website:

MATTHEWRIEF.COM

ONE

FIRST, YOU SET the stage.

Dozens of intricate pieces methodically positioned like a line of dominoes. Each carefully selected and timed to perfection. Organized and meticulous. Backups and contingencies in place. Redundancies, alibies, and fake reports, all ready to go.

The hooded figure sat in a dark room, staring across a spread of three computer monitors, his mind firing with rapid, expert precision. His pulse slow, and his eyes focused. This wasn't his first rodeo, but the stakes had never been this high. Not even close. But he was ready, prepared, and poised for what he was about to do.

He checked everything again, then double- and triple-checked. There was no flaw—none except the variable accounting for human error. But he'd even prepared for that.

He pictured his plan coming together like a brilliant work of art or a dazzling symphony. It would be his magnum opus—his masterpiece. And with the click of a mouse, he tumbled the first domino, leaned back, and grinned, waiting for the world to burn.

FLORIDA STRAIT

Commander Sharpe awoke to the sound of knuckles rapping against the door of his quarters at just past zero two hundred. It was relentless. A constant barrage that prompted him out of his rack in a blink.

He stepped to the door and cracked it open.

A young lieutenant's face was coated in a thin layer of sweat, and his words rushed. "We've picked up an unidentified object, sir. Your presence is needed on the bridge."

Sharpe was already across his quarters and sliding into his coveralls and zipping them up. Less than twenty seconds after the words had left the tactical action officer's lips, Sharpe's boots were laced tight, his cover was on his head, and he was out the door.

They rushed forward to the combat information center while the lieutenant explained the situation as quickly as he could. Watchstanding sailors looked back at their commanding officer, their expressions displaying disbelief as he strode into the dimly lit space. The CIC aboard the USS *Nitze* was humming with the usual activity of computers, monitors, and fans, but a loud, rhythmic beeping sound also filled the air.

A petty officer second class adjusted her glasses before leaning forward and pointing at a tiny blip that had recently appeared on the right side of her radar screen. It was moving fast, pulsating its way west from the Berry Islands in The Bahamas. And it was flagged as "unknown."

Sharpe and the TAO closed in from behind as the sailor swiftly calculated the object's speed at just over six hundred miles per hour. The 3D radar estimated its altitude at just three hundred feet above sea level. At that rate, the object would cut across the upper portion of the Florida Strait and reach the mainland in fifteen minutes. And if it maintained its current course, it would make landfall in the heart of Miami.

"Where did it first appear?" the commander said, his eyes narrowed as he stared at the screen.

The second class radarman pointed to a spot on the upper portion of the monitor, halfway between the midpoint and the right edge.

"The speed and size fit the profile of a medium-range cruise missile," she said, her tone laced with intensity.

Sharpe nodded, then turned and strode out of the room, forward into the bridge, the object being tracked while he called higher-ups in his chain of command.

Utilizing Aegis, the US military's combat system that integrates radars and computers aboard the warship to track and engage enemy targets, the *Nitze* locked onto the mysterious missile.

Sharpe promptly made contact with a joint task support team at the Pentagon and was informed that the unknown object had also been recently picked up by Coast Guard and commercial ATCs on the mainland. The commanding officer was given the green light to engage.

Ending the brief call, Sharpe gave the order to ready two SM-6 missiles via the ship's vertical launch tubes. The order was executed, and word was relayed from below deck that the missiles were ready less than twenty seconds later.

All eyes not on the radar displays were on the commander, who, after taking a deep breath, gave the order to fire the first missile.

A hatch opened just in front of them on the main deck. A plume of white smoke and a twenty-foot rocket blasted out, tearing through the quiet night air and screaming a thousand feet up before leveling off and flashing northwest with a long trail behind it. The missile swiftly reached its top speed of just over twenty-six hundred miles per hour.

The bridge fell perfectly silent, all eyes fixed to the monitor as the nation's first line of defense streaked across the sky, homing in on its quarry.

TWO

WEST TEXAS

JASON WAKE HOVERED his right hand over his holstered pistol as he eyed the five armed men fanned out in front of him. It was near pitch black in the enclosed space, and the smell of gunpowder and charred brass hung in the air.

He twitched as a faint series of clicks punctured the room, followed by a hiss.

Suddenly, and without warning, lines of dim lights flashed on, and his adversaries scattered in different directions.

Jason snatched his Glock 21, slid it free, and raised it chest-height while bending his knees. The action was rapid and smooth, and by the time he had his weapon leveled, his chosen target was lined up in the sights.

He pulled the trigger. The weapon kicked back, and the .45-caliber round burst free, blasting through the heart of the digital apparition and causing it to vanish. He let loose a second in rapid succession, taking down another three-dimensional projection before leaping to his left and rolling for cover behind a metal barrier.

An ear-piercing siren blared from the corners of the room, and red flashing lights beamed in chaotic circles as the lights at the corners dimmed. Jason poked his head around the side, then turned and popped up, already aiming at the nearest target. He fired twice more, sending bullets right through two of the holograms.

His movements were surgical. Precise. Honed by thousands of hours of practice and intensive study, training each and every muscle to work in unison with his mind, and making the pistol an extension of his body. Never satisfied and always striving for perfection.

With the final digital adversary taking cover at the back of the room, he rolled right and closed in with his weapon raised.

Waves of fog hissed from vents in the floor, swallowing him up and obscuring his view of his target. He crouched lower and adjusted his course, breaking free from the haze at his enemy's flank. But his target was nowhere in sight.

Turning around, he scanned the mist-covered room, searching for movement. It came in the corner of his eye—the digital apparition appearing from the haze, weapon raised. Jason beat the hologram to the punch, adjusting his aim with smooth, expert precision, and firing and taking down his final target with a strike right through the head.

The image vanished. The siren and flashing lights cut off, and the hissing ceased, replaced by a fan that cleared the fog away.

Jason stood and relaxed and ran a hand through his black hair. He smiled as he surveyed the scene, then took a step toward the middle of the room. The moment his boot struck the floor, the lights darkened again, and three more figures appeared, spread out like a triangle right in front of him. All three opened fire the moment they materialized.

Jason hit the deck as fast as he could but wasn't quite swift enough. One of the automatic rounds pelted him in the left shoulder, sending a sharp charge of electricity across his body. He winced and rolled, then popped up behind cover and fired three rapid shots—different lines, and each pull of the trigger a fraction of a second apart.

The digital figures disintegrated, and Jason let out another breath. He had six rounds still in the magazine, one in the chamber, and all enemies down. But he scowled as he eyed his left shoulder.

The lights died, drowning the space in perfect darkness for a moment. Then they flashed on bright, and a door opened at his back, followed by the sound of heavy boots striking the slick concrete.

Jason turned and focused on Marcus Chapman. Though shorter and leaner than Jason's six foot three, two hundred pounds, Marcus was intimidating. The middle-aged black man was all muscle and intensity. A thirty-year veteran of the Army Green Berets and former Delta Squad commander, Marcus had been running the covert training facility for the past five years.

"Care to offer an explanation?" the hardened military man said.

A handful of explanations flashed into Jason's mind, but none of them good. "Got complacent," was all he said.

"Two words you'll never hear a soldier say after returning from battle. You know why?"

"Because the ones that got complacent are dead."

"Damn right they are. I don't care if the instructions stated there'd only be five adversaries. The enemy won't follow any sort of rules. Understand? You win or you die." He stared straight into Jason's eyes, then gestured behind him. "Time to get cold, Wake."

"Yes, sir."

Jason handed Marcus his pistol on the way out.

He rushed from the simulation room, down a set of metal stairs, and into the twenty-thousand-square-foot pool area. In the center was an Olympic-sized swimming pool that was forty feet deep at one end. The state-of-the-art pool had powerful jets along the sides that could churn the water into a frothy, bubbly mess designed to make even the best swimmers helpless. It also featured a wave generator that could send out large, crashing rollers.

Around the main pool were smaller ones for various other training purposes. They could simulate all sorts of situations like deep-water escape and evasion tactics—incidents covert operatives might find themselves in.

On his way across the space, Jason passed a crane suspending a sedan over the deep end of the main pool. Half a dozen trainees treaded water near the edges while instructors prepared the exercise, teaching them how to escape a sinking vehicle.

Jason went straight for a circular pool in the corner and splashed in without hesitating. The water was frigid, barely a degree above freezing at all times. It sent a powerful shock through his body the moment he entered, igniting his senses and hastening his breathing.

The covert facility was unlike anywhere else on Earth. Known simply as Tenth Circle, or Dante's

Tenth Circle of Hell, the program was created by top veteran Special Forces, CIA, and FBI agents. It was a brutal curriculum that began with weeks of excruciating workouts to weed out those who lacked the necessary mindset. The regiment transitioned to more technical facets, but the physical aspect never let up. There were hours of running up and down the canyon walls, swimming with bricks over their heads, pull-ups, pushups, and planks. It never ended at Tenth Circle.

And Jason was experiencing a brand-new addition to the program.

"No one comes back to Tenth Circle," Marcus had said after Jason stumbled up to the middle-of-nowhere facility for the second time in his life.

But Jason wasn't short on demons, and the best way he knew how to keep them at bay was by pushing himself to the limit—physically and mentally—and focusing his energies elsewhere. And for him, there was nowhere better to accomplish that than Tenth Circle.

Jason treaded in the icy water for five minutes, which, to him, felt like an eternity. Marcus sauntered up, grabbed a rubber brick from the deck, and lobbed it into the pool beside Jason.

"Retrieve it," Marcus said.

Jason didn't hesitate. He'd learned long ago that when it comes to doing painful but necessary things, hesitation is the worst enemy. At ten feet, it was far shallower than the deep end of the big pool, but the distance felt far longer as he forced his body through the biting liquid—his mind racing back to his recent incidents in Iceland, where he'd been swept away by a subglacial river.

His body shook, and his heart thumped audibly as he grabbed the brick and brought it back to the surface.

Marcus ordered him to continue treading water, but with the brick extended high over his head. After another five minutes, and three more brick retrievals, he was ordered back into the simulation room. The cold exposure made the difficult exercise infinitely more so—creeping right to the border of impossible. But that was the purpose of it all. Jason had been taught again and again that oftentimes the enemy isn't the main issue. It's the variables. Being able to operate while undergoing a high level of pain, cold, fatigue, and confusion.

"You have to be able to perform at your best, even when you're at your worst," Marcus always said.

That was the main message at Tenth Circle. Everyone who stepped through its doors knew how to shoot and lay out an adversary. The program enticed some of the best Special Forces soldiers and agents in the country.

Jason did the simulation twice more, then he hustled down for more cold treatment before returning for yet another batch of exercises. It was all about perfection—fine-tuning every little movement. No wasted energy. Nothing done without a reason. Nothing random or unplanned. Everything methodical. Shaving off fractions of seconds here and there until the weapon retrieval, target acquisition, aim, and firing were completed perfectly.

After hours inside, Marcus thought Jason could use a good warming up. He ordered him to the grinder—out through the doors and into the relentless Texas sun and blasting heat. There, Jason ran up and down the canyon until Marcus got tired of watching.

And so it went for months on end. From dusk 'til dawn. Intense and unforgiving and utterly exhausting. Relentless training for the day when shit hit the fan—for when the nation's fate hung in the balance and the highest caliber of operatives were needed. The day when the world stood still and waited, on the cusp of catastrophe, needing a miracle to prevent everything from spiraling out of control.

And three months after Jason had returned to the classified crucible, that day arrived.

THREE

SCOTT COOPER WOKE to the chaotic sound of a buzzing phone. He propped onto an elbow and reached for his nightstand. As he did, his eyes glanced over a digital display showing two thirty in the morning.

The former Navy SEAL commander and current covert operations squad leader had two cellphones. One for everyday use, which he kept on silent at night, and a second durable flip phone he always kept within arm's reach and never silenced. It was his emergency line, and he could count on one hand the number of people who had easy access to it.

He cleared his throat, tried to blink the tiredness away, then answered. "This is Cooper."

Ten minutes later, after kissing his sleeping wife on the forehead, he was dressed and climbing into a black BMW parked in his garage. He flew down the nearly empty streets to Miami International Airport, flashing his ID badge at the private terminal entrance and gassing straight onto the tarmac. He stopped beside an idling Jayhawk Coast Guard helicopter, then hopped out into the morning drizzle.

A suited man ushered Scott toward the chopper's open side door. "Your team's nearing the site, Mr. Cooper." He handed the covert leader a folder marked classified. "Read this on the flight. Good luck, sir."

It was clear to Scott that the senior government agent had no idea what was going on but could feel the unusual gravity of the situation.

Scott gripped the folder, holding it close to his chest to keep it dry as the Jayhawk's rotors sped up. He kept low, shielding his face from the wind as he hustled into the bird.

The R/V *Valiant* tore north through the Florida Strait, the two-hundred-foot marvel of maritime engineering pushed to its blistering max speed of sixty knots. No expense had been spared in its design and construction. Though by outward appearances, the *Valiant* looked like an ordinary research vessel, it was secretly one of the most advanced ships on the planet. And that was why her crew had gotten the call.

They'd been on their way to the Berry Islands in The Bahamas to investigate the mysterious deaths of four European tourists and two dive operators from New Providence who'd lost their lives during a recreational dive. But they received a call, and their course had changed just after two thirty in the morning.

"Helicopter's inbound," a comm tech in the bridge said.

Alejandra Fuentes nodded, the tall, athletic Latina all-focus as she gazed out the forward windows. A former special agent, Alejandra had been one of the first people recruited to join the unique covert group, and she possessed skills that not only set her apart in combat situations, but also made her an effective third-in-command. Seeing behind the curtain and eventually realizing firsthand the level of government corruption in her home country of Venezuela—and with Scott and Jason offering an opportunity unlike any she'd heard of before—she'd signed up.

"Distance to search zone?" she said, eyeing the radar techs.

"Five minutes at our current speed."

The timing matched up nearly perfectly. The *Valiant*'s three Rolls-Royce waterjet engines eased them down to a crawl to keep the vessel steady in the current as the Jayhawk tore in from the west. It swept in smoothly and descended toward the helipad at the bow. The research vessel was equipped with advanced ballast systems, allowing it to remain steady even at high speeds or while sustaining substantial swells, so the pilots performed the landing with ease.

Scott Cooper climbed out, marched into the superstructure, and ascended two levels to the command room just aft of the bridge. It was a small space with a table and chairs and monitors along one of the walls.

Alejandra and Kelvin "Finn" Castro, the group's engineer and diving specialist, were waiting for him when he arrived.

The moment he entered, Scott said, "Status of the submersible, Finn?"

"Warmed up and ready to swim," the short Latino said.

Scott bobbed his chin. "Search systems online?"

"Yes, sir," Alejandra said.

"Good. Begin the sweep. Keep us at ten knots for the first pass. I want all hands on deck and alert. We can't miss this thing."

Finn tilted his head and shrugged. "What exactly are we looking for?"

Scott's emergency phone buzzed again. He answered immediately, then gave the order to power up the main monitor for a secure video call.

"We're about to find out," Scott said as the screen came to life. He slid the classified folder from the inside of his coat and set it on the table. "More questions than answers in there."

The call connected, and the room fell quiet as the image appeared before them. They gazed at four serious middle-aged men in military dress uniforms sitting around part of an oval table—members of the Joint Chiefs of Staff, including the chairman and the chief of naval operations.

"Mr. Chairman," Scott said, his voice loud and articulate. A former senator, in addition to being a distinguished Special Forces operative, the man could stand before a group of the world's elite and make a speech or charge into enemy fire without a pinch of nerves. "We've arrived at the designated search area. Two Coast Guard cutters and a Navy destroyer are also nearby."

"Your sonar's up and running?" said Chief of Naval Operations Admiral Arthur Gears.

"That's affirmative. We're operating with the widest swath, and our magnetometers are powered up as well. If something's down there, we'll find it."

"Good," said Chairman General Ken Richardson. The highest-ranking service member in the US military cleared his throat, then added, "This will take no more than three minutes, as that's all we can spare. At zero two hundred this morning, an unidentified object was caught on radar by air traffic controllers at our Coast Guard base on Inagua, in The Bahamas. Less than a minute later, the same object was picked up by radar systems aboard the destroyer USS *Nitze*, both confirming a westward trajectory, an altitude of three hundred feet, and speed of six hundred miles per hour. The object was deemed hostile, and the *Nitze* engaged, firing a single SM-6 missile that successfully intercepted the threat and blew it out of the sky. We're confident this was an organized and premeditated attack. What we need to know is what kind of missile it was so we can figure out an origin and intent."

Scott nodded, having listened intently and taken mental notes. "We'll find the wreckage, sir."

Scott ran through the details in his mind. Given the low altitude and speed, and the radars that first picked up the attack, he concluded right away that it had to have been a cruise missile, most likely mid-range.

If it had been an intercontinental ballistic missile, the rocket's heat signature would've been picked up by NATO ballistic missile defense infrared satellites prior to it even leaving the atmosphere. Word of the launch would've spread like wildfire across worldwide NATO assets, and efforts would've been made to take the missile down prior to its reentering the atmosphere.

The chairman verified Scott's conclusion, then gave the missile's believed specifications.

The reality, and close-to-home nature of the surprise attack, hit Scott hard, but he didn't show it. The projectile had been over twenty feet long—a cruise missile no doubt capable of carrying both conventional and nuclear warheads. And it had been shot down just fifty miles from the Miami coastline while Scott slept in his warm bed, alongside his wife, with their two daughters just down the hall.

"Any leads on where it was launched from?" Scott said, doing his best to keep his anger in check.

"Yes," the chairman said, "but we'll be keeping that on a need-to-know basis for the time being, Mr. Cooper. Just let us know what you find."

"Yes, sir."

The call ended, and Finn slid over a laptop he already had open to a GPS image displayed. There was a red circle that blossomed out from their current position, the shade getting lighter the farther it went.

"This is the search area we were sent," Alejandra said.

The *Nitze*'s radars had been tracking the unknown missile on impact, and a team of analysts had predicted where to find the bulk of the wreckage. The specialists had obviously been precise, as less than thirty minutes after the video call ended, they picked up remnants of the missile on sonar.

"Looks like some decent hits," Finn said as the crew watched the sonar display in the bridge. He stepped closer and pointed at the screen. "There are pieces spread out all over the seafloor, but this section looks to still be mostly intact.

"Hundred and forty feet down," Alejandra added, checking a monitor that displayed various parameters.

Scott folded his arms and narrowed his gaze. "Time for some answers, Finn."

FOUR

IN THE EVENINGS, Marcus and Jason would occasionally spend time in an advanced training room, competing in intense games of target acquisition. They'd watch film of terrorist attacks and compete to pick out the bomber or shooter prior to the incident. They'd trained to keep a sharp eye on physical cues and pick up on unusual and suspicious patterns in body language.

No one had ever officially completed training at Tenth Circle. The program didn't have a set end point. Operatives were released when their respective government organizations needed them back. But Jason had come as close as anyone, so Marcus had to create and add new modules to the curriculum. He'd never had a student like Wake before.

The two of them had grown close, Marcus taking on a sort of father-figure role in Jason's life. Though Jason had grown up in the lap of luxury, his father, a corrupt billionaire businessman, had been abusive and rarely present during his upbringing. And Jason had accepted his inheritance for one purpose: to try and right some of his father's wrongs.

Though Jason and Marcus had become unofficial friends at the covert facility, Jason had never seen the inside of the veteran's office. None of the trainees had. So it took Jason by surprise when he was awakened early one morning and ordered to report to the top floor room known as the "crow's nest."

Jason laced up his shoes, splashed ice-cold water on his face, then toweled off and hustled up three flights of stairs. He reached Marcus's office and rapped his knuckles on the door.

"Come in, Wake."

He entered and saw his mentor wearing shorts and a T-shirt, his hands on his hips as he gazed through tall windows toward the pool area below. Jason did a quick survey of the room. There were rows of medals and awards on his desk and a side table covered in challenge coins. Pictures on the wall depicted scenes from various eras, some with presidents, and some with Marcus's family.

"You ready to leave yet?" Marcus said, the man watching intently as a dozen trainees were ushered into the pool area below.

"Why do you always ask me that?"

He shrugged. "What's the point of all this training if you don't put it to use?"

"I have. You know that."

"Not lately you haven't. You've been here three months." Marcus rubbed his chin, then turned to look at Jason. "Unless . . . you're here for other reasons. You know, there are better avenues for coping with one's past."

"Everyone has their ways. This is mine."

Jason's past was a shadow-riddled enigma that both infuriated him and motivated him with such fierce intensity that he was able to routinely push himself right to the edge of his limits. It hadn't even been two years since his fiancée had been murdered in an act of terrorism—a suicide bombing that took place right before his eyes. Then, Charlotte Murchison had been injured while saving his life, the renowned archaeologist still on life support in a coma at George Washington Hospital in Washington, DC.

Jason felt responsible. The powerful demons of his past demanded powerful restoratives, and Tenth Circle was Jason's remedy of choice.

He eyed the medals and coins once more. The plaques, awards, and certificates were remnants of a legendary career, the accolades of a patriot, if there ever was a man fitting of the title.

"I've heard talk you might be retiring soon," Jason said.

"Let's stay on subject."

Jason's gaze drifted from the accolades to the framed pictures. The ones nearest to the desk were close-ups of a baby and a toddler.

"Your kids?"

Marcus chuckled. "No shortage of flattery . . . Grandkids." He motioned toward a picture farther down the line of two adults. "Those are my kids. And they're older than you."

Jason nodded.

Marcus studied the young operative, then shook his head. "I've still never been able to figure you out, Wake."

Jason ignored the remark and said, "A prototype of our team's new extraction drone should arrive any day now for testing." He leaned back, then glanced over his shoulder, staring in the direction of the simulation room two walls and a floor away. "And those AI systems could use an upgrade, you know. They've just innovated these new—"

"Your charitable donations to the facility are appreciated. But dammit, kid . . . You gonna make me say it?"

Jason eyed him quizzically, and Marcus just sighed.

"You could be the best fighter in the world, but what the hell's the point if all you do is train? The world needs you. And not in the middle of nowhere, Texas, testing out new gadgets and gunning down digital combatants."

Jason stiffened. "I'm ready, and I'll be ready to answer whenever I'm needed. Until then—"

"Well, you're needed," Marcus interjected. "Scottie called. There's apparently been an incident. Big and serious."

"What kind of incident?"

Marcus shrugged. "I've got a top-secret clearance, but only on a need-to-know basis." The hardened military man eyed Jason again. "A chopper's picking you up in a couple hours. Zero six thirty."

Jason checked the time, then scanned the room again. "I guess we'll have to finish this talk next time I come back."

"There won't be a next time." Marcus turned away from him again and stepped toward the glass. He stared down as the trainees splashed into the pool, instructors yelling and spraying them with water. "Come on," he said, motioning toward the door. "You and I are going for a little run. There's something I want to show you before you go."

FIVE

FINN POWERED ON the submersible's exterior lights, the powerful beams flashing ahead and illuminating nothing but clear ocean as far as they could see. Alejandra sat beside him in the surprisingly spacious interior of the advanced underwater vehicle. Ahead of them was a big, circular glass window offering hundred-and-eighty-degree views of the subsea world.

"Beginning our descent," Finn said into the radio, then he vented the sub's ballast tanks.

Air released overhead, bubbling to the surface as it was replaced with seawater to reduce the vehicle's buoyancy, and they began to sink.

Just minutes earlier, they'd been lowered into the water via the *Valiant*'s moonpool and were descending right on top of the largest portions of wreckage picked up by their sonar.

Less than fifty miles east of Florida's Gold Coast, the visibility was nearly perfect, and despite dropping toward a depth of a hundred and forty feet, it wasn't long before the seafloor came into view. It appeared mostly flat and sandy, riddled with the occasional ridge and patch of rocks.

"There," Alejandra said, pointing to the left seconds after the bottom came into view.

Manning the controls, Finn powered on the thrusters and angled the craft so the forward lights illuminated the spot she was pointing at. They descended and closed in more, Finn having to combat a steady two-knot current. The pillars of light washed over part of a cigar-shaped object that was broken apart, its exterior blackened from the explosion that had shot it out of the sky.

Finn motored in closer, keeping a good distance from the bottom and moving slowly to prevent swirling up clouds of sediment.

They hovered right beside the wreckage, scanning the light across its entire exposed exterior.

"Well done," Scott's voice said through the speaker, the covert leader observing their activity via the sub's onboard cameras. "We're working to create a digital replication of the missile so we can figure out who made it. See what other wreckage you can find."

"Copy that, Scottie," Finn said, then eased the craft into a three-sixty rotation, shining the powerful lights across the seafloor in all directions.

"There." Alejandra pointed again when the sub was halfway into its rotation.

Finn chuckled. "I'm making a mental note to never play I spy with you." He closed in on another piece of the wreckage, this one smaller but more intact than the last. While sweeping across it so Scott and the team on the Valiant could get a 3D image of the missile, Finn noticed numbers along one of its sides. He pointed it out, then exchanged glances with Alejandra.

"You really think it would have identifying markings?" she said.

"Hey, it's a missile, right? It's supposed to blow up. Why would it matter under normal circumstances?"

The man had a point, but despite his angling the sub and lowering it as close to the bottom as he could, they couldn't see the whole series of numbers and letters.

"You think you could lift it up a little?" Alejandra said.

"Way ahead of you." Finn programmed the sub to remain steady with the current while grabbing the controls for the vehicle's robotic arms. He extended the two limbs out from the body and reached forward. Sliding the pincher hands into the sand beneath the wreckage, he tilted them around, then lifted. When the object wouldn't budge, he throttled up the thrusters to give them more lift, the powerful little rotors spinning nearly full speed to provide enough thrust.

The wreckage lifted, giving the team a clear picture of not only the missile's identifier, but also an Iranian flag.

Ten minutes later, Scott was on the phone with Chairman Richardson.

"You're sure it's Iranian?" the general said.

"Positive, sir," Scott replied. "We ran the scans of the wreckage through our software just to be sure, and it came back a perfect match. It's an Iranian cruise missile."

General Richardson fell silent a beat.

"What is it?" Scott asked, knowing he was overstepping his bounds but feeling he needed an answer.

The chairman cleared his throat. "We were afraid you'd say that." He sighed and then returned with even more authority in his voice than usual. "An Iranian cargo ship was heading toward the Atlantic, right where the missile was first picked up on radar."

SIX

MARCUS AND JASON started out on the well-trodden paths, zig-zagging sections of grit pounded as hard as concrete from thousands of bodies running up and down them. The paths were a testament to the training at Tenth Circle—years of sweat and effort, all right before their eyes, striking shoes managing to reshape the landscape.

They continued along for a quarter mile and half a dozen switchbacks, then veered off along the rim. Marcus led the way. Jason didn't know where they were going. He'd never left the paths before, always wary of the instructors' watchful eyes criticizing their every move.

Marcus led him along steep portions of the canyon walls, where the path was barely noticeable. They followed the lines rainwater had flowed and created over the years, little cuts in the landscape swirling down toward the rushing river below.

After another half mile, they began to ascend again, this time approaching the crest of an apex in the ridge. A raised overlook. The going was slow and tough, and it seemed like every other step, Jason was slipping on the loose pebbles blanketing the rough earth. And even with the sun out of sight, the temperature was over seventy degrees. The air was dry and offered not a breath of wind. The desert is no place for sissies, and that's especially true in the arid regions of Texas, where the mercury routinely climbs into triple digits.

The sun was just about to peek over the flat stretch of nothingness to the east when the going steepened even more.

"I got a crisp Jackson says I'll beat you to the top," Marcus said between quick gasps.

Jason responded by cutting sideways and picking up his pace, charging right alongside his mentor. They scrambled up the rugged terrain, both breathing heavy and grabbing at the rocks and parched weeds to keep from tumbling into the canyon below.

Pushing with everything he had, Jason just managed to pull ahead, summiting the apex less than a stride length ahead of Marcus. Both of their shirts were soaked in sweat as they stopped to catch their breath. Reaching into his pocket, the veteran soldier slipped out a twenty. Jason waved it off, but Marcus stuffed it into the young man's pocket.

"I'll get it back," Marcus said, then pointed toward the corner of the edge. "This is Jayla Overlook. I named it after my wife, and it's the only word fitting for a sight so beautiful."

Sharp cliffs flanked the narrow plateau on three sides, and Jason looked around, taking it all in. The view from the facility was by no means bad, but from that vantage point, he could see a hundred miles in every direction. The horizon was flat and barren aside from the winding canyon and winding river at its base, curving down from the distant mountains, sluicing perfectly east for about twenty miles, then gradually bowing south. He couldn't see it, but he figured it had to continue even more down the line, due south, to eventually meet up with the Rio Grande.

From there, Jason could barely make out the exterior shape of Tenth Circle nestled along the top of the canyon to the east. It was only because he knew it was there that he could see it. The structure blended in nearly perfectly with its surroundings. Besides the covert facility, there was nothing on the horizon that hadn't been there for thousands of years. No sign of human life.

Marcus sucked in a deep breath of air. "You know what this canyon's called, right?"

Jason nodded. He'd heard talk among other trainees during his first spell at the facility.

"Do you know why it's called Chrome Canyon?" Marcus added, then continued before Jason could attempt an answer. "It was named by the founders of this facility. Because Chrome, by itself, is incredibly hard but brittle and easily broken. It's used as an alloy and is therefore only as strong as the elements it's combined with. Just like the operatives we train. Just like any soldier in the history of mankind. You're only as good as your team, and you can't do everything alone. You can't fight every battle by yourself. Even the ones in here." He tapped a finger against Jason's forehead, then turned away. "Especially the ones in there."

Jason gazed out over the expanse before him, letting the words sink in.

"You asked me yesterday whether or not the rumors are true that I might be hanging it up soon," Marcus said. "Thirty years in the Army, Wake. Nine deployments. Six duty stations. A total of thirty-five years and seventy-three days of service to this nation has taken me away from my family. I've missed so much. So many things I can never get back. I'm not going to do the same with my grandkids."

Jason smiled. "No one's earned a rest more than you."

"Who said anything about resting? I'm not dead yet. I have no clue how to live in a world that isn't this, but I'm going to figure it out. The same way I always do . . . through conscious effort. Through planning and focus. Trial and error. Unknowns have never scared me before, so why should this new one be any different?" He nudged Jason's shoulder. "Anyway, it's up to you now. It's your generation's turn to take the reins."

Marcus turned to gaze to the west, watching as the sun glowed up in a steady, rich ember, setting fire to the dry, flat world and streaking beams of intense light through the canyon.

Jason eyed the man he admired as much as anyone alive.

You're a great man, Marcus.

He wanted to say it. The words were right there on his lips, but Marcus let out a loud breath and turned before Jason could give them a voice.

Marcus checked his watch. "Your ride's gotta be on its way from Laughlin." The veteran Special Forces soldier scanned the canyon wall, tracing a line back to Tenth Circle. "But before you go, and before I hang it up, I've got one more order of business . . . Beating your cocky ass in a footrace. Double or nothing back to the grinder."

Marcus took off, leaving Jason in a cloud of dust for a moment before the young operative grinned and gave chase. Jason planned to take it easy, to shift up to third gear and click on cruise control, giving the man his final victory. But he didn't need to. After they'd descended the steep portion and reached the barely noticeable path, Marcus took off. The man lived up to his legendary reputation and left Jason in his dust, once again.

Pumping his arms and fighting to remain balanced on the unforgiving, untamed landscape, Jason pushed as hard as he could, but he couldn't close in. Marcus was moving like a man possessed, with perfectly timed strides and cuts and leaps.

The air was heating up faster than an oven as the sun climbed higher. Beads of sweat pooled and dripped down Jason's face, soaking his hair and shirt. Instead of a leisurely cruise, he was in his highest gear, fighting with all his strength, and still, he could see nothing but the powdery dirt lingering in faint plumes.

Forcing up a steep shortcut, Jason finally managed to cut the distance between them. Marcus was twenty yards ahead, flying along the ledge at a blistering pace. They reached the outer stretches of the main pathways, then cut upward, tearing their way up the switchbacks.

While wrapping up a sharp turn, a distant sound filled the air, overtaking the rasps of air rushing in and out of Jason's lungs and the pounding of his soles against the earth.

Helicopter rotors, he thought, not taking his eyes off the back of his mentor. *My ride's early.*

He didn't dare glance at his watch, but he knew it was true. They'd made phenomenal time heading back.

The rotor noises grew louder, flying in fast, then more resounded, low and buzzing softly—not the violent, powerful chomps of a Sikorsky or a Bell, but something much smaller.

Jason finally stole a glance over his shoulder. Marcus did the same as they approached a section of rock marking another sharp turn up the opposite direction. And just as they turned, ear-rattling pops filled the air.

"Get down!" Marcus shouted.

A faint glare of tiny dark spots in the sky, nearly blotted out by the morning sun, came into brief focus before Jason did as he was ordered. With no time to slow, he rolled onto the hard-packed earth, tumbling over the edge and dropping ten feet to a stony slant alongside Marcus as a burst of heavy-caliber bullets battered the canyon walls beside them.

SEVEN

THE RAPID FIRE of high-caliber rounds clapped across the steep valley like lightning—incessant, booming cracks shattering the stillness.

Jason rolled forward in a blur of noise and confusion. Rounds pelted the rock behind him, spitting up puffs of dust and grit. He landed on a sharply angled slope, colliding with a long stretch of loose rocks that gave way on impact. He slid down a small avalanche of loose shale, dust clouding around him and blotting out the sky.

The gunfire persisted, echoing off the rockfaces and into the distant horizon.

Jason caught buzzing noises, as well, intermixed with the ear-piercing shots. They were drones, and they were closing in even more, zipping toward them over the canyon. There was no time to wonder who was attacking them and why. At that moment, they were exposed and caught severely off guard.

Marcus landed right beside him. They both struggled to balance as they rushed down the steep gradient, their legs buried by the retreating rocks.

"There!" Marcus shouted, motioning toward a wall of rock ten feet high, stuck along the side of the canyon like a scab.

Ignoring the pain from the landings, they both dove and rolled and slammed against the rockface, just beating the barrage of gunfire pummeling the ground behind them.

The firing stopped for a moment, and the buzzing of rotors and whirring of intricate electronics filled the air as the drones moved in and spread out. Jason peeked over the rock and caught his first glimpse of the unmanned vehicles. There were three of them, roughly the size of dining tables, and each had four rotors that branched out from a body loaded with an array of cameras and sensors, as well as a mounted automatic rifle.

Marcus also eyed the three aircraft, then looked toward Tenth Circle. The facility was less than a quarter mile away from them and was quiet as a tomb. The nearest doors were sealed shut and blended in with the brown and tan terrain.

"Something's wrong," Marcus said. "The defense system should be kicking in. These drones should've never gotten close without us spotting them."

The buzzing sounds grew louder, and the two peeked up just as the three drones whirred back into view. They were spread out and sweeping in with a maneuver that would make them both exposed in a matter of seconds.

They pressed themselves against the slab, and Marcus led Jason at a daredevil pace, shuffling around the jutting rock. On the other side, the walls opened up again, revealing a sharp slope.

Marcus stabbed a finger ahead, pointing at a narrow slit in the canyon wall up ahead. "We've only got one shot at this."

The moment he rounded the corner, the veteran took off, running full speed along the steep canyon. Jason followed, barely able to make it three steps before gravity pulled him down.

They slid and tumbled down the fragile rocky slope while fighting to keep their momentum driving forward. By the time they reached the opposite side, they were stumbling nearly out of control on the loose surfaces. They pushed and dove and rolled before barging into the shadows of the crack.

"This thing runs nearly all the way to the base of the facility," Marcus gasped as they climbed up a steep edge and into the winding crevice that was barely two feet wide at parts.

Jason kept his peripherals alert to the crooked strip of crisp blue skies above as the sounds of the drones buzzed circles like angry hornets.

One soared overhead then looped back, its camera locking onto the slit in the rock, and the barrel of its weapon training into position.

"Get down!" Jason yelled, diving and tackling Marcus to the dirt.

The two landed hard and rolled under the natural arc of the crevice wall as the successive rattling of bullets barked across the frontier once more. Rounds blasted shards of rock and peppered the area inches from their bodies as the two army-crawled their way through the final stretch of the cave.

The drone whined and looped back, vanishing from view.

"They're regrouping," Marcus said. "Preparing for us to pop out and make a run for it."

Jason scanned the walls of rust-colored sandstone that nearly enclosed them. "We could wait them out. Their batteries won't keep them airborne forever."

Marcus nodded, and the drones circled back toward the spot where they'd entered the slit.

The two of them climbed and peeked around a corner, catching a better glimpse of the western edge of the covert installation. It was still perfectly silent—no alarm blaring, no armed operatives flooding out, no countermeasures of any kind.

"This is wrong," Marcus said, shaking his head. "An attack here is unlikely, but we've got protocols in place. The facility is on lockdown, but there should be reinforcements out here to protect the—"

"Three o'clock!" Jason said as he spotted movement.

Marcus turned, then his eyes bulged when he saw three soldiers moving along the top of the ridge less than a hundred yards away from them. They were all wearing ghillie suits, the light-tan camouflage garments allowing them to blend in perfectly with the desert landscape when not moving. From that far off, the three looked like giant tumbleweeds sliding along the terrain, but their rifles were sticking out, the barrels parallel with the dirt and aimed in Jason and Marcus's direction. The three armed men swiftly cut between them and the facility, then turned and closed in.

"Shit, change of plans, kid," Marcus said, sliding back down for better cover. "Waiting out the mosquitoes is a no-go. And we're not getting back to the facility. Not with pistols against long-range rifles in that exposed terrain."

They both looked around, then Jason eyed a tight opening in the crevice near their feet. "Where does that go?"

Marcus shrugged. "I don't know, but there's light far down there, so it's gotta open up."

They cooked up a quick plan, then split up. Jason backtracked in a fast crawl through the crevice while Marcus squeezed into the constricting space and vanished down into the darkness.

The air was stuffy and hot as Jason pushed through. He did his best to remain composed—to keep his heart rate in check and remain focused on each individual task instead of the sum of their parts.

Soon, he rounded a sharp bend and spotted the opening back out onto the steep rockface coated in loose stones. The drones were nowhere in sight, but he could hear them circling. Their sounds echoed, bouncing off the canyon walls and seemingly coming from all directions.

He crept out of the hole and into the light, pausing every few seconds to look around. He was exposed, and he was about to be even more so as he eyed a ledge branching out over the cliff face.

He took a half step back as one of the drones hovered into view. It banked around, vanished, and then another appeared ten seconds later. They were fanned out, forming a triangle and rotating over the last place they'd seen the two men. Jason waited as the nearest drone passed, knowing he'd need to be quick if he was going to pull off his role in their plan.

The moment the drone swept out of sight, he climbed along the ledge, then was forced to inch along with his hands before reaching a five-foot gap. He took in a deep breath, tightened his gaze, then dug his shoes into the warm, smooth rock, and then shoved off, hurtling his body across the gap. He struck at a weird angle, and his body wanted to twist, but he forced his arms against the corner and caught, gripping with his fingers as tightly as he could. His right gave way, but his left managed to hold firm long enough for his feet to dig into holds and steady his body.

He remained perfectly still, hanging suspended over the cliff with his body pressed to the crag as a drone soared around. He stole a glance skyward, watching as the unmanned vehicle flew past. It felt like ages, and the moment it vanished, he heaved himself up onto the flat surface and sprang forward into a crook of shadow.

He took cover again as another drone passed, looking up as it zipped by. It was faster than the others—there one second and gone the next—its swivel camera training across the top of the crevice and the barrel of its weapon tracking the movement.

It vanished, then another appeared, also streaking swiftly. The changes in speed would make his role in the plan more difficult.

Jason withdrew his weapon and prepared for the next drone to complete its trajectory, giving him a clear shot at its underbelly and its fragile, vital components. But as he took aim, the tone of the rotors shifted. The powerful motors whined, and the three drones regrouped, tightening closer before ascending and fanning out again.

Jason peeked around once more, catching his first look at their new positions. They were easily a hundred yards above, and he watched as they dispersed again and continued their rotation and search.

Or they're falling back to cover foot soldiers.

He pictured the three men in ghillie suits. They'd be closing in by then and getting into position. Maybe gearing up to lob a grenade into the crevice to force him and Marcus out of hiding.

Movement startled Jason. He spun left and raised his weapon, focusing as Marcus crawled out into view fifty yards along the canyon wall. Covered in dust, the hardened Special Forces veteran came to his feet and got his bearings. He noticed Jason nearly instantly and threw a quick nod his way.

This was it. Make a move now, or forever hold your peace.

Jason stepped back, dropped to a knee, and took aim toward the blue above, focusing on the buzzing aircraft high overhead. He picked one out and homed in, trying to anticipate and lead it like a quarterback hitting a receiver darting a cross route. Locking in and keeping steady, Jason exhaled and fired five shots in rapid succession.

EIGHT

THE FIRST THREE shots streaked wide, the target far and cutting fast from right to left across Jason's partially obstructed field of view. The fourth struck home, sparking against one of the rotor assemblies, and the fifth missed. The little vehicle jolted and spun wildly on its axis. The damaged rotor sputtered, throwing the craft off balance and sending it into a spiraling free fall.

Mere seconds after Jason let the rounds loose, the drone burst into pieces in a powerful explosion and vanished in a vortex of flames that seemed to vaporize the aircraft.

As Jason watched the scene unfold, the other two drones shifted trajectories, cutting around in a blink and flying full speed toward his position. He dropped and pressed his back to the wall of rock, his weapon ready, his eyes trained to the skies, listening as the little aircrafts whined closer.

Based on the sounds, he figured they were both descending as well as sweeping toward him, preparing to take him from both sides at once and from mid-range.

Jason swallowed and prepared, looked left and right, needing to make another move. He lowered himself even more, then crawled into a corner to make his profile as small as possible. He took aim where he figured they'd first appear, readying his finger on the trigger.

The drone to his left reached him first, but just as it soared into view, gunshots thundered across the backcountry once again, coming from the east down along the canyon. A rapid volley of six shots. Two struck the craft, both sparking into its body, and the little vehicle flew into a chaotic spin, jerking up and down before tearing apart in a sudden explosion just like the first one had.

Jason spotted Marcus lying prone, his upper body the only thing visible, poking out from a tiny opening in the rock.

Jason spun around, ready to engage the final drone. They were no longer outnumbered by the unknown aircraft, and with his finger on the trigger and his eyes narrowed, he readied himself to finish them off.

But the final drone shifted its trajectory again. Turning on a dime, it cut back and rose high into the air, then Jason spotted new movement coming from his right. The three men in ghillie suits appeared out of nowhere, rushing down the side of the canyon. They crouched and took aim with their long-range rifles while the drone circled rapidly for a closer shot at him.

Jason's body took over. He darted for his only means of escape. Lunging east, he threw himself over the side, soaring onto another edge of loose rocks and tumbling before forcing himself to his feet and booking it along the unsteady terrain.

He stumbled behind a massive boulder, then cut around, unable to stop himself before rolling right to the edge of a sheer drop. His pistol jarred free as he forced his hands into the crag, clawing to stop himself on the steep gradient. Stretching out his body, he scraped to a stop with his legs dangling over the edge, his hands gripping whatever they could on the smooth rock face.

The river roared at his back a hundred feet below, and he clawed at the rock, grunting and digging deep. Managing to force his right shoe into a hold, he muscled himself over the edge and came to his feet just as Marcus appeared. The man came to an abrupt halt in a cloud of dust ten feet away.

Just as the two locked eyes, the final drone appeared, buzzing around the canyon to Jason's right. It stopped in a blink, hovering less than twenty yards away, its camera and rifle barrel locked onto Jason.

The young covert operative raced through his options. Marcus still had his pistol, but he didn't have a shot—not from behind the boulder. And Jason was unarmed, his weapon resting on the edge five feet away.

Jason stood frozen, the sound of shuffling men in the distance—the camouflaged soldiers with rifles closing in.

He had no choice but to dive for his pistol and try and take a shot at the drone. He was going to die. He was certain of it. Even okay with it. Maybe Marcus could escape while he briefly distracted their enemies.

Less than a second after the standoff began, Jason bent his legs and prepared for his final move. Just as he was about to go for it, Marcus rushed toward him in a blur and dove out from the shadows. Before Jason could react, Marcus crashed into him, colliding and hurtling them both toward the edge.

The drone opened fire, pounding a streak of automatic rounds as Marcus shielded Jason's body. The projectiles blasted through flesh as the two men tumbled over the cliff, then soared toward the raging waters below.

NINE

THE HOT AIR rushed by as Jason spun into a free fall, whipping faster and faster as he accelerated in a chaotic, bright blur. Squinting, he fought to straighten his body, hoping he wouldn't strike the side of the canyon.

Jason suddenly reached the bottom with a powerful, resounding splash, the water smacking against his legs and sending a shockwave up his body as the river swallowed him whole. He sliced sideways after breaking through, and his feet thumped against the rocky bottom. The torrent grabbed hold and dragged him, throwing his body shoulder-first against a smooth rock and sending him into a violent tumble.

He opened his eyes. It was murky, and he could barely catch glimpses of light. He kicked and pulled at the water, breaking free to an unrelenting roar that amplified across the bottom of the canyon as he sucked in a deep breath.

He fought to steady himself as he scanned the sloshing, white-capped surface for any sign of his mentor. Piercing cracks ripped across the sky, overcoming the rumbles of the river. A bullet screamed past and splashed beside him like a meteor. It was followed by two more in rapid succession, the rounds barely missing his exposed body as he jostled along the raging waterway. The men in the ghillie suits were opening fire, though he couldn't see them that far down in the canyon.

Jason sucked in a deep breath and dropped down, forcing himself deeper. He exhaled and remained submerged as the river twisted and turned. It was over ten feet deep but narrow at most spots, so Jason felt every curve as renegade boulders pounded into him from the haze, sending him into spins and throwing him off balance just in time for his body to strike the next underwater rock.

He stayed down for what felt like an eternity. His lungs throbbed, and his body ached from the back-to-back collisions. He kicked and rose, breaking free again and taking in a breath. As he looked around, the canyon appeared the same, and the rising sun made the desert landscape blinding, the rays sparkling off the water and canyon walls with such intensity he could barely see anything. But he was out of range of the gunmen—that much was clear. Gazing skyward and back toward the west, he couldn't see any sign of Tenth Circle or the winding trails up the steep slopes.

He swept over the turbulent waters once more for any sign of Marcus. He hadn't seen his mentor since the man had tackled him over the cliff and sent them flying down the canyon.

"Marcus!" he yelled, his voice overpowered by the sounds of the river. "Marcus!" he called out again, this time giving it everything he had.

The name echoed off the rockfaces, then died away. He kicked right to avoid a jutting rock, then turned back and scanned as much of the river as he could see. The gushing stream straightened out and widened, and Marcus came into view. He was in the river, floating face-down and motionless.

Jason gasped as he tore at the water, splashing as fast as he could toward his mentor and friend. He reached Marcus halfway down the straightaway, and after grabbing hold of his body, Jason heaved him around. The first thing he noticed were two gruesome bullet holes. Blood soaked his clothes around the wounds and dyed the river crimson.

Jason fought to keep Marcus steady, but they both slammed into a submerged rock, breaking apart a moment before Jason could regain his control. He grabbed Marcus again and held his head up. He was cold and lifeless, and his skin was already draining of color.

"Marcus!" Jason yelled a third time, tapping the man's face.

He didn't want to check for a pulse. His world was already tearing at the seams. Finally, he pressed a finger to the base of Marcus's neck. Nothing. The man was dead in his arms.

The walls of rock closed in again, and the river transitioned to rough twists once more. As Jason lifted his finger away, a familiar humming sound echoed through the gorge. Jason looked back as the drone descended straight toward him.

He took in a quick breath and forced himself down again, going with the unseen turns in the river as the drone swooped down and fired a line of rounds across the river, splashing a straight trail. Jason could hear the gunfire and even saw one of the bullets as it torpedoed through the murk right beside him.

A painful realization grabbed hold. With Marcus's body floating right above him, Jason would never be able to escape the drone. The quadcopter could hover right overhead and wait, and the moment he appeared, riddle him to pieces, as well. To survive, Jason would need to leave him. He'd need to abandon the revered war veteran and let his corpse float alone down the river.

With no other choice, Jason turned and kicked for the side. He reached ahead with his open hands until they grazed rock, then he contorted himself around and jammed his shoes into a corner and held on tight. He tucked deeper, trying his best to keep himself steady against the relentless wall of water. It rushed past, trying with all its strength to tear him away, but he held secure, waiting and biding time for what felt like an eternity.

His lungs throbbed again, but he waited even longer, ignoring the pestering discomfort. The water seemed to grow stronger and louder—the throbbing in his lungs more convincing, then screaming. Nearing the verge of blacking out, he let go and kicked. Splashing back into the bright, loud world, he took in much-needed breaths, his eyes focusing on the skies above. As he'd hoped, the drone was gone, but as the canyon wound farther along, he could hear it. The walls eventually parted again, and he spotted the unmanned vehicle hovering over the river fifty yards ahead. It was facing away from him and tracking Marcus's corpse.

Jason dropped down again as the device circled up and back, scanning the area from a higher vantage point. Again, Jason managed to grab hold of an underwater corner of sandstone, the water pulling at his body and the force driving the rock into his fingers.

When he resurfaced the second time, the drone was even farther along. He repeated the shallow free-dives twice more, then the drone was gone entirely.

Jason remained vigilant for another thirty minutes, keeping his eyes trained skyward, watchful for any sign of movement, and ready to drop back down at a moment's notice. He knew the device couldn't follow him forever, and after half an hour without another visual, he figured he'd made it.

But he was far from home free.

One of the biggest reasons for Tenth Circle's location was its extreme isolation from human activity. It was situated in one of the remotest parts of the country. An area so unpopulated, it's still referred to as "frontier"—hundreds of square miles of nothingness, and no roads near the covert training facility. Far from the eyes and ears of anyone who might see it and question what it was. It was nearly impossible to find unless someone already knew it was there.

That had been the idea, but someone *had* found it. Someone who wasn't supposed to.

As he navigated the rough, unforgiving waterway, his mind played back the attack—the sudden, decisive, well-organized attack. His face tightened as he thought about it, then he felt a surge of anger as he pictured Marcus. He pictured the patriot posing with his family in the photographs covering his walls.

Jason had no way of knowing who'd attacked them, but one thing burned certain in his mind: he'd figure it out. He'd make it out of that remote river, and he'd discover who the culprits were. He'd track them down to the ends of the earth.

And then he'd make them pay for what they'd done.

TEN

JASON THREW THE attack out of his mind for the time being, along with the pain he felt from seeing Marcus's dead body.

He needed to get out of there.

While riding along the tumultuous river, traversing miles through the canyon, he tried to picture the world around him. Three times he'd flown in a helicopter to Tenth Circle, each trip taking off from Laughlin Air Force Base and soaring two hundred miles over the tan, barren terrain. He hadn't seen many roads, and none during the final leg of the flights.

It wasn't until the sun was a quarter of the way along its arcing trajectory that Jason spotted a bridge spanning the gorge up ahead. It was the first one he'd seen. The first manmade object of any kind.

The bridge was decrepit, with weathered beams, missing planks, a rusted frame and struts, and a damaged foundation that gave it a substantial tilt barring its use. It looked like nothing with an engine had crossed it since Kennedy was in the Oval Office. Jason figured it was built by optimistic miners or oil barons, looking to strike it rich via one buried commodity or another.

A quick peek at his watch told Jason he'd been flowing down the river for nearly two hours, though it'd felt like an eternity. It always does when there are other places you'd rather be. Other places you need to be. When you feel like there are so many things you could be and should be doing, but there he was, stuck and useless.

He ran the rough math in his head. He'd once read that the fastest rivers in the world travel up to seven miles per hour, and moderately fast ones hover around three miles per hour. And he guessed he'd been traveling at a speed somewhere between those two. That meant he'd floated around ten miles downriver. To the east at first, then bowing to the south. The sun was almost right over his left shoulder. He figured the river would stay on its southerly course until it dumped into the Rio Grande.

Regardless of how far he'd traveled, Jason was sick and tired of staying still, of just floating along. It wasn't the way he liked to live his life. He preferred to grab it by the reins and wrestle it into submission, than be passive and wait for everything to fall into place.

So, despite the condition of the bridge, Jason decided it was time to climb out and take a look around.

Once in the shadow of the bridge, he kicked left and grabbed hold of a boulder. Figuring his pursuers would be running the same calculation he'd done to estimate his distance from Tenth Circle, he waited there a couple minutes.

And soon, he heard a far-off engine, echoing from the northwest and growing louder. Then the sounds stopped, and he spotted one of the guys in a ghillie suit. He'd removed the top half of his camouflage—the sweltering heat having taken its toll—and gripped a high-powered rifle with a scope.

The man stepped up to the rim and pressed the rifle butt snug to his shoulder and used the scope to scan the river from the distant bend to the line of shadow caused by the bridge. He was far off, and the glare from the sun was blinding, but Jason caught flashes of his face, which was mostly covered by a thick, unkempt beard.

Jason watched as the guy scanned the riverbed one more time, then the top of the canyon edges, then the flat expanse surrounding him in all directions. He lowered his rifle and said something into his radio, then turned and disappeared. The vehicle's engine grumbled again, and it drove off, heading back to the west.

Jason waited until the sounds vanished on the horizon, then he scanned the shoreline and let go of the boulder. He floated another thirty seconds, then picked the friendliest gradient and kicked for the edge, grabbing hold of the shore and pulling himself from the jaws of the river. He rolled onto a flat, hot rockface and regained his bearings before scaling the wall.

It was much steeper than it'd looked from the water, and there were no paths. No signs of humans ever climbing down.

He reached the top, and the moment he stood at the summit, a blast of hot, choking air rushed into him. The river had been refreshing and kept him cool during the journey, but now he was feeling the full brunt of the Texas heat.

He shielded his face from the sun and gazed northwest first, looking for any sign of his attacker's vehicle. When he didn't see anything on or around the nearby hills, he shifted his eyes, following the line of the barely noticeable dirt road. To the north, it stretched away from the bridge like a faded carpet, seemingly into eternity, and fizzling out on the boiling horizon.

He surveyed the road across the other side of the bridge. Same thing. Just a long, lonely stretch of dirt. No signs or turns.

Jason trekked along the rim and climbed onto the angled bridge, stopping in the middle. The planks were warped, slightly arcing over the ravine and giving him a couple more feet of vantage. But it didn't help. The road reached out forever in both directions.

As he scanned back, he noticed a bright spot to the east, far off in the distance and nearly perfectly adjacent to the bridge he was on. He estimated it was roughly four miles away and slightly north of his position. It was too far to make out what it was, but the brightness and size told him it must be a structure of some kind.

Going for it was a gamble. It could very well be a structure, but it could be abandoned. Life wasn't exactly booming in that part of the country. It could also be a lot farther than four miles. Flatness and heat and wide-open terrain have a knack for tricking your mind.

Jason took a minute to run through everything, then decided to gamble. He took off into a steady jog that amped up unconsciously with each stride, while the temperature seemed to rise a degree every second. Soon, the full force of the day was bearing down on him.

He'd traversed five hundred yards when a bullet soared past his head and pounded into the dry earth right in front of him.

— — —

The hitman was using an Accuracy International long-range rifle, a full magazine locked in position and packed with five .300 Winchester Magnum cartridges. He was clutching the weapon when he spotted Jason running across the desert far in the distance, their offroad SUV having looped back around after not seeing any sign of their quarry.

He ordered the driver to brake and shut off the engine when they were two hundred yards from the bridge.

"We can't make it across here," the driver said, pointing toward the damaged bridge. "We'll need to find another route."

The hitman climbed out and strode toward the canyon with his rifle. "We don't need to cross."

He watched Jason carefully, keeping his eyes locked on their running target as he climbed up onto the bridge and carefully made his way to the highest point in the middle. Once there, he knelt on the old planks and rested the barrel on a rusted truss.

The powerful rifle was equipped with a Vortex Razor scope, a versatile optic device that allows its user to focus on targets that are both close and far away and works well to combat glare in bright conditions. The experienced assassin pressed his cheekbone against the butt stock, closed his left eye, and focused his right through the optics.

He put Jason in his crosshairs, then gauged him to be roughly a quarter mile away and getting farther with each passing second. He was also bouncing a little and turning left and right to avoid the occasional dried shrub. It was a far-off, difficult shot, but plausible for a top marksman, and he'd always been one of the best. Even as a kid, in Royal Marine basic training, and all the way up the training ladder with near-perfect marks, and that was why he'd been chosen to be a sniper. But anger issues, a bad temper, and problems with authority don't mix with the military. A folded chair to the side of his superior officer's head had put a swift end to that short career, and so here he was, lining up his sights on a target for a big payday.

The hitman adjusted the scope, then calmed his breathing and hovered his finger over the trigger. Keeping calm and steady was the key—any oscillation, no matter how minuscule, would have a drastic effect down the line. A tiny fraction of an inch becomes a ten-foot miss at that distance.

The wind was the biggest varying factor. It was gusting from time to time but hovering around ten miles per hour and blowing in from the south, sweeping right across his quarry. This meant he'd need to aim significantly to the right of his target to compensate, in addition to aiming high to account for gravity's pull on the bullet.

And so he picked his target position, performing quick calculations in his head and without the help of a spotter.

Less than thirty seconds after he got into position, the professional was ready. He steadied the reticle, waited for the calm pause after an exhale, and then pulled the trigger on the downbeat of his heart.

The round burst from the barrel with a powerful kick of the weapon. It took half a second for the bullet to travel the distance, and the hitman observed carefully as it struck nothing but dirt, flying just over his target's right shoulder.

The man made a rapid adjustment, chambered another cartridge, and fired again, anticipating Jason to respond to the first shot instinctively and drop into a momentary crouch before diving for cover. But instead of crouching, Jason used the brief moment to dive immediately to his left. The second round finished its brief flight three and a half seconds after the first one and also struck nothing but dry earth.

By the time the hitman adjusted for the third shot, Jason was out of his sight. The professional cursed softly to himself while scanning his crosshairs over the terrain. After a minute, he zoomed out for a broader view and then waited.

"He can't lie and wait forever," he whispered to himself. "And he's not gonna crawl a couple hundred yards. Not in this heat."

He pictured his prey lying prostrate and inching along the scorching desert, his hands burning and body roasting.

With his eye focused through the scope, he waited patiently. He was good at waiting—the simple yet invaluable skill having paid dividends for him for years.

Three minutes after vanishing beneath the blankets of mesquite, his target returned. Jason sprang to his feet fifty yards farther away and to the right of where he'd dropped down. He rose right into a sprint, darting right for thirty feet before abruptly cutting back left, zig-zagging away from him.

The assassin lined up as best he could. With his target moving randomly from side to side, he let loose a third quick shot, narrowly missing his target.

He remained calm and observed, doing his best to guess for what he knew would be his final window of opportunity. Jason was now seven hundred yards away, an incredibly difficult shot without wind and with an unmoving target. But the hitman had never failed to take down a target in his sights, and he wasn't going to start today.

He put Jason in his crosshairs again, ran the calculations, and made the adjustments while studying his target, trying to predict his future movement.

He let out his breath once more and pulled the trigger. It missed left, the distance nearly perfect, but Jason had shifted just before the round struck. He loaded another round, took aim, and fired immediately. The assassin's final shot tore through the air, and his target went down, vanishing beneath the shrubs.

A smile formed on his face as he gazed out at nothing but desert terrain, seeing no sign of movement. He waited there for thirty seconds, then rose to his feet. The driver, who was also wearing just the bottom half of his ghillie suit, strode over.

"It's done," the sniper said, striding confidently off the bridge.

The driver stared to the east, then shook his head just as the sniper passed. "No, it's not."

The sniper gazed over the landscape, spotting blurry movement far in the distance. He used the scope to focus and watched as Jason resumed his race across the desert.

"Son of a bitch," he said.

"There are backup mags in the truck," the driver said.

The sniper shook his head. It wasn't happening. Not there, anyway. What minuscule window had existed was now closed, but the guy who'd hired them was thorough and cautious. He always worked contingencies into the fold, and for this operation, there were two of them: He and his men were plan B.

Striding back toward the vehicle, he slipped out his radio and called plan C.

ELEVEN

JASON BOOKED IT full speed, cutting sharply left and right to avoid the sniper fire. Being unpredictable was key, so he performed swift changes in speed and direction.

His unknown attacker was using a bolt action rifle—that much was clear based on the roughly three-second intervals between shots. After a series of shots missed, he changed up his movements again, and then hit the ground once more.

The fifth shot whooshed right overhead and was followed by a long pause. Suspecting his attacker might be thinking his shot had landed, he crawled for a full minute before jumping to his feet and taking off again. Jason resumed his rapid, zig-zagging escape for another minute before easing back slightly and straightening his course, locking in on his faraway destination.

Needing all the pushing he could muster, he thought back to the encounter and used it as fuel as he pounded across the hard, parched landscape. Fortunately, his estimation had been wrong in his favor. The heat and boiling ground had made his objective appear farther away, and he closed in on the shining structure just under three miles from where he left near the bridge.

Just as his clothes had dried from the water, they became soaked with sweat instead. And his breathing was rushed when he stopped and shielded his eyes again and squinted at his destination. Wiping beads of moisture from his brow, he made out more details of a square-shaped building and the area surrounding it. There was a truck parked off to the right, and as he moved even closer, he realized it was a small gas station nestled alongside another road, this one paved.

Jason picked up his pace again, and just as he reached the faded pavement, he spotted a vehicle approaching. It was far off but moving fast.

The gas station had two pumps and a red sign that read "TJ's." The structure he'd seen was a garage, big and rusted, beside a convenience store. He could see a man standing behind a counter and eyeing him through a dirty window.

Jason cut across the old lot and pushed inside, relishing the wave of cool air provided by an AC unit buzzing audibly in the corner.

The man behind the counter just stood there staring at him. Jason figured that a guy who worked in no man's land had probably seen some unusual things. He figured not a lot would phase him.

Up close, the guy looked older and rougher, with leathery skin, gray hair, and a tough aura—like he'd just stepped out of a black-and-white Wild West flick with John Wayne.

"I need to use your phone," Jason said, striding across the room.

The guy had his right hand underneath the counter. "The phone is for paying customers. You a paying customer?"

"I don't want trouble." Jason didn't have time to waste. He considered leaping over and disarming the guy, then he patted his pocket and slipped out the damp twenty Marcus had given him earlier that morning. He unfolded the note and set it on the counter. "Two Gatorades. You can keep the change if you give me the phone."

The guy's suspicious gaze remained as he streaked the bill toward himself. He peeled it off the counter, then handed over a phone and returned his right hand to whatever was mounted under the counter.

Jason eyed the keypad. There were a lot of people he could call. A lot of people who'd give him an ear and dive into action.

He punched in a series of digits and placed the handset to his ear. An answer came on the second ring, as if the person on the other end was hoping to receive a call from an unknown number with a Texas area code.

The call lasted thirty seconds, then he hung up and checked his timepiece. Ten minutes 'til pickup. The sense of urgency amplified in his mind. Shit had hit the fan, and powerful people were scrambling.

The man pointed to a refrigerated section at the back of the shop. Jason made his way to the fridge, grabbed a Gatorade, then emptied its contents down his parched throat. He grabbed a second and chugged it as quickly as the first, then as he stepped back to the counter, a vehicle pulled into the lot out front.

Jason gazed out the same windows the shop owner had eyed him through as a dirty black SUV with tinted windows braked to a stop. It remained idle a moment in front of the pump.

Jason sighed, then eyed the owner. "You good with that shotgun?"

The man hesitated a moment, then said, "This is Texas. And the nearest police station isn't exactly down the street. Yeah, I'm damn good with it."

Jason knew there was no way to convey to the guy that he was a highly trained American covert operative who'd been honed into a weapon to fight vile men around the world. That he'd been at a secret covert training facility spontaneously attacked by an unknown, powerful enemy. That he was involved in an urgent matter of national security.

But even if the guy would've believed him, there wasn't time for all that. Because the moment the words left the owner's lips, the SUV swooped around and parked parallel with the front wall. The back left door opened, and two pairs of boots appeared in the open space of the undercarriage. The men kept behind the vehicle, then one of them crept toward the hood, the other toward the rear fender, both wielding pistols.

Jason didn't know who they were, but he knew they sure as hell weren't the police. He stepped back and crouched behind the corner of the counter.

"You gotta get out of here," he said to the owner.

The man grabbed his shotgun and pumped a shell into the chamber. "Like hell," he spat as if he was back at the Alamo. "Like I said, we're far from the nearest station. Where am I gonna go?"

Jason focused on the SUV and the two men at the corners, weapons raised and waiting.

"I'm not armed," Jason said.

"Good. For all I know, you could be with them, robbing my place. This could be your MO."

Jason motioned toward the brand-new Escalade that retailed for over six figures. "Do these look like guys who stick up gas stations for a couple hundred bucks?"

"You could be with them," he spat again.

The guy at the rear of the SUV vanished, then reappeared, hurling a baseball-sized object toward the store window. It punched through, shattering into the shop. Shards rained down as the grenade revealed itself, smacking into a rack of magazines before tumbling off the counter and toward the floor where the owner was.

The man cursed, threw himself over the counter, and landed beside Jason as the device blew. It was a frag grenade and exploded with an ear-piercing pop that hurled hundreds of jagged shards of metal in all directions. The projectiles pounded into the counter and ceiling and shattered the windows.

"Shit," the man said, crawling up to Jason and pressing his shoulder to the counter beside him. "I fought in Vietnam. Damn thing just took me back there."

Jason stared into the man's eyes. "Still think I'm with them?"

The man shook his head, then removed a Colt revolver from his hip holster and held it out to Jason.

"I'll take the twelve gauge," Jason said, peeking toward the parking lot. "That way you can cover me with the pistol."

The man handed over the shotgun instead.

Jason checked the chamber, then ran through scenarios. "We're gonna split up," he said. "Then on my signal, provide cover."

The man nodded, then Jason counted to three. When he finished, the two peeled away, the owner heading for the back, and Jason diving in between rows and rushing to the far side of the space. He swiftly managed to reach the corner and took cover behind a chest freezer.

Just as he turned back to look toward the SUV, the power in the store cut off. The lights went out, casting the space in shadows, and the humming AC unit sputtered to a stop. He guessed the outside electrical box was somewhere along the side, which meant one of their attackers was flanking them and heading for a back entrance.

The act clicked on a mental timer in Jason's mind. Seeing the two men still huddled behind the SUV, he shuffled around and made eye contact with the owner. Jason gave him a signal, and the man poked out of his hiding place, took aim with his Colt, and opened fire with three powerful rounds. The sudden booms shook the space, the gunpowder igniting and launching masses of lead through the glass and into the SUV's frame. He hadn't been lying about being a good shot. Though supposedly cover fire, the bullets struck precise points near the rear and forward sections of the SUV and even punched through the passenger window, allowing Jason to see a man hunched in the driver's seat.

The two guys taking cover dropped back, then the rear guy inched forward to meet up with his buddy. The lead one poked around the hood, his pistol aimed. He fired right away, bursting rounds toward the entrance and pelting bullets into the counter shielding the owner. Both men were now exposed—nice targets from Jason's position.

In the middle of the attackers' barrage, Jason aimed through a break in the glass at the closest guy and blasted the first shell. Hundreds of pellets ricocheted off the front end of the SUV and ripped across the guy's body. Jason fired another shell, striking the second guy's exposed shoulder just before he disappeared.

Immediately after firing the second shot, Jason dropped down and darted back across the store, his mental timer continuing to count down. He slid across the sleek floor and crouched beside the owner.

"There a door back there?" Jason said.

The man nodded. "Leads to my shop."

"Okay, now you take the left vantage." Jason held out the shotgun and motioned toward the front left corner of the store.

The man exchanged weapons with Jason and broke away. Gripping the revolver, Jason crawled toward the back, stopping at the open frame and peeking into the darkness. He caught a glimpse of the back door that was less than an inch open.

Shoving the Colt into the back of his waistband, he grabbed a car battery from the back counter, whirled around, and swung it into the open door just as a man appeared. He was low and in an athletic stance, his pistol forward. Caught off guard by the attack, the man tried to jump away, but the heavy object caught him in the side, pounding into his body and throwing him off balance.

Jason burst inside, grabbed the guy by his gun hand, and hurled him into a wall. The man fired chaotically as Jason fought to relieve him of his weapon. Just as Jason ripped the pistol free, the guy headbutted him in the cheek, nearly putting him down.

Jason stumbled to a workstation. Throwing open a drawer, he grabbed a hammer as his adversary closed in from behind. Jason whirled around and bashed it into the guy's shoulder. The man yelled and dropped, then Jason knocked him out with a kick to the head. He went limp, his body draped over a yellow mop bucket.

Jason didn't waste a second debating his next move. The moment the man hit the cold floor, he bolted across the room, heading for the back door.

"Cover fire!" he yelled, then slipped out the door.

The heat blasted into him, feeling even more intense than before.

The owner fired two shotgun shells toward the SUV as Jason pushed through the stifling wind, threaded passed piles of stacked auto parts, and cut around the side of the station. He put himself into the mind of his attackers: what were they going to do next, and what did they think he was going to do next?

These were professional hitmen. The guy in the back had experience fighting hand to hand, and they'd rolled up with grenades in their SUV, which meant they probably had a lot more toys in the vehicle. He figured that, seeing their flanking man hadn't made an appearance in the store, they'd taken a moment to reevaluate. Maybe chuck another explosive into the store. Maybe call in backup. Either way, Jason planned to slice their plans to shreds.

Jason poked around the corner, his weapon raised. The shop owner's firing had subsided, and the guy near the rear of the SUV was unclipping something from his waist. He shuffled backward in his crouch, then reared back another grenade. Jason fired a round before he could hurl the explosive, his bullet striking the guy in the hip at an angle just below his vest and bursting out his lower back. The man stumbled backward, releasing the grenade and letting it tumble along the other side of the vehicle.

It blew, and thick sprays of gas hissed out. The man scrambled away from the toxic cloud, retreating to the right side of the vehicle as Jason sprinted away from his cover. He managed to cut the distance in the brief confusion, throwing his shoulder into the guy and bashing him against the back of the SUV. Jason struck the guy across the face, then pinned him to the frame and blasted a round into his foot.

As the guy fell, he jammed his elbows down, slamming the bone into Jason's right wrist and knocking his weapon free. But with one foot disabled, the guy was toast. Jason landed another blow to his face, then threw him headfirst into the rear window, his skull punching through the thick glass and resting lifeless.

Jason hit the ground as the driver swiveled back and fired sporadic shots through the glass. Creeping along the right side of the SUV, Jason was halfway down when the first guy he'd shot appeared. He was limping, and blood blossomed from all over his body.

Still disarmed, Jason instinctively grabbed the rear door and slammed it open, striking the guy and causing him to stumble back. Again, the driver took aim, forcing Jason to drop and allowing the other attacker to recompose himself.

In a split second, the injured man raised his weapon. Jason turned and tried to reengage the man, but he was exposed and too far off. An explosion filled the air, a wave of pellets pounding into the base of the bloodied man. The guy jolted and fell back, flailing against the dirt.

Jason didn't look right, but he knew what had happened. The shop owner had had a clear shot, and he hadn't wasted it.

A mechanical click caught Jason's attention, and he dove into the back seat of the SUV as the driver put the vehicle in gear and mashed the gas pedal. The rear tires squealed, fighting for traction before getting their grip and rocketing them forward. The force threw Jason against the seatback, and the door slammed shut moments after his impromptu entrance.

The driver roared the vehicle across the lot in a blink. He glanced over his shoulder and dropped his jaw at the sight of his unwanted passenger. Turning sharply, the driver bounced the rig onto the main road and accelerated. The force threw Jason across the seat, and the driver kept his left hand tight on the wheel while reaching back with his right.

Jason steadied himself and caught the guy's wrist as he opened fire. The shots were deafening in the tight space, and the rounds punched holes across the roof. The ringing in Jason's ears was painful as he squeezed tighter and surged forward, jostling the weapon free. He rolled over the center console and into the passenger seat, then pressed his back to the passenger door and threw his heels into the guy.

The speedometer raced up past fifty, the endless road stretching out ahead of them. Another kick caused the guy to jerk sideways and turn them sharply to the right. When Jason launched out of the seat and into the guy, they turned even sharper, flying off the road and bouncing onto the rough terrain. The grill whacked against sporadic undergrowth, and the frame jostled at the high speed.

Seeing a hill coming up through the sea of mesquite, Jason threw a palm into the guy's nose, then leaned forward and yanked on the driver-side door handle. Shifting back, he slammed his heels once more, ejecting his final adversary from the vehicle. The man tumbled out and vanished from view. A loud thump resounded, then the SUV shook wildly out of control.

Seeing a tower of rocks up ahead, Jason contorted his body and struck his foot on the brake. The big, heavy vehicle protested. The brakes whined, and the SUV slid sideways, coming to a rough stop less than ten feet from the boulders.

Jason sat still a moment, catching his breath. He scooted into the driver's seat and then turned the SUV around, driving in the direction they'd come. He found the driver a hundred yards back, bleeding and motionless, his body sprawled out unnaturally over a large cactus.

Jason motored back to the gas station, the beat-up vehicle barely making it. As he stepped out and walked back into the store, he passed the two bodies and the spent tear gas canister, its contents having hissed away and blown off in the wind. The sounds of distant, powerful rotors caught his attention, and he gazed to the east, then relaxed and headed inside.

The store owner, still wielding his shotgun, was standing by the door when he entered. Jason gave him a quick nod, then headed to the back. He found his unconscious attacker in the middle of the space, his wrists and ankles wrapped in laps of duct tape.

Jason grabbed a bottle of water from the refrigerated section. He felt the cool of the liquid and the already building condensation on the exterior as he uncapped it and strode into the back room. He downed half the contents, then doused the rest over the guy he'd put to sleep. The sudden rush of ice-cold water splashing against his face caused the guy to jolt and his eyes to spring open. He breathed erratically, then froze when he saw the pistol aimed at his face.

"You're going to tell me who hired you and why," Jason said, gripping the weapon and narrowing his gaze.

The man blinked as water flowed off his face, and then he adjusted his position. He stared back at Jason, studying his face. "You have no idea how screwed you are, do you? Cipher is on the hunt. Your fate has been sealed." A devilish smile formed on his face. "If we don't kill you, others will. You've been marked, Jason

Wake. You've been marked, and there's only one way this ends for you."

Jason wasn't given a chance to ask another question. Just as the final word left the hitman's lips, he rotated his jaw and bit down, cracking an object with his teeth. By the time Jason grabbed hold of him, the man was already convulsing, and ten seconds later, his body went limp.

TWELVE

THE SOUNDS OF the helicopter became deafening as it circled around and descended onto a flat patch of earth beside the store. Flurries of dust howled back from the powerful rotors, crashing into the outside of the structure like a passing sandstorm and flurrying through the shattered windows.

"Friends of yours, I hope?" the shop owner said, still gripping his shotgun as the bird dropped down to the pavement.

Jason nodded, then extended a hand. "Thanks for having my back." He motioned to the damaged storefront around them. "And I'll take care of all this."

The guy sighed as he eyed the place. "Hard to run a gas station in this condition."

"What's TJ short for?" Jason said, squinting through the shattered windows and reading the sign in front of the establishment.

He gave a blank expression. "Tuck Jackson."

"Well, Tuck, it's a good thing you're about to retire." Jason made no explanation. He just left the Colt on the counter and stepped out, shielding his face from the gusts of dirt as the rotors slowed. The side door opened, and Alejandra Fuentes stepped out, the beautiful Latina wearing sunglasses, tight tactical pants and boots, and a short-sleeved shirt with a bulletproof vest.

She surveyed the scene as she approached Jason. "Area clear?"

Jason shook his head. "There's at least three more still out there. Along with a remaining drone."

Two government agents climbed out behind her. Jason gave them a quick rundown of what happened and told them about what the owner had done.

"Local police are on the way, along with FBI field operatives," one of them said. "We'll stay behind and wait for them, then clean this thing up as best we can."

"There are search helicopters on the way, as well," Alejandra said. "They'll sweep these hills for the others."

Jason climbed aboard. Alejandra sat across from him, and they both donned headsets as the pilots throttled the engines back up and lifted them off the ground.

"You look like hell," Alejandra said as she handed Jason a bottle of water.

Jason grabbed it but made no reply. His clothes were soiled and dirty. He had deep swelling on the side of his face, and his body ached from his ride down the rapids and diving onto the hot desert.

"What's the status of Tenth Circle?" Jason said.

"Perfectly fine, far as we've been informed. The facility wasn't touched, and all hands are accounted for. Aside from you and Chapman. Any idea where he is?"

Jason fell silent, then lowered his head.

Alejandra clenched her jaw. "I'm sorry to hear that. I've heard amazing things about him."

Jason stared out the window, using the time to think over everything that had happened. He wasn't surprised that Tenth Circle hadn't been touched. After all, the hitmen weren't after the covert facility. They were after him. The fact that he'd been hunted down after the initial surprise attack had solidified the conclusion in his mind. Then the guy back at the station knew his name. It wasn't a terrorist attack or military operation. It was an assassination attempt.

"We're flying to Tenth Circle now," Alejandra said. "See what we can dig up before heading to The Bahamas."

"Bahamas?"

"Yeah. Scott wants us back there. Trust me, it's the bigger fish right now."

"I'm not going. I need to figure out who did this."

Alejandra made no reply. They fell silent for a solid two minutes before curiosity got the better of Jason.

"What's going on in The Bahamas?"

Alejandra unconsciously peeked over her shoulder, as if someone could overhear her words on a chopper flying over the middle of nowhere in Texas. She gave him a succinct version of what happened and what the US's response had been so far.

Jason sunk deeper into his seat and became quiet again, his mind blotting out the rest of the world.

"You guys found the missile?" he eventually asked.

"What was left of it. Then Scott sent me here to get you. The whole thing became more urgent."

"Well, don't leave me in suspense."

"It was a Hoveyzeh cruise missile," Alejandra said. "Made in—"

"Iran," Jason said, rubbing his chin. "Turbo-jet engine and capable of low-altitude flight. Range of eight hundred miles, I believe."

"Right. And it's believed to have been fired from an Iranian cargo ship. The vessel was off course and right where the missile was first detected."

Jason thought again. "It's a relatively small missile and could've been stowed in a shipping container."

"There were three crew members on board when the ship was found and seized." She checked her watch. "There was a jurisdiction issue, but they should be being transferred to an interrogation facility near Miami within the hour. Hopefully, they can give us some answers."

"Is the *Valiant* still at the missile wreckage site?"

"Apparently, they're heading east to search the area where the missile first appeared on radar. Investigating a hunch, Scott said."

The moment their destination came into view, Jason's thoughts homed back on the task at hand. The chopper descended onto a flat patch of desert thirty yards from Tenth Circle's eastern entrance. It was the same helipad he'd landed on twice before, both times before meeting Marcus at the entrance.

There were three other helicopters parked nearby and dozens of agents roaming the grounds, along with armed soldiers. They were all combing the surrounding paths and brush for any clue as to who the attackers were.

Jason and Alejandra headed straight for the agent in charge, a veteran FBI operative named Ferguson.

"We've only been on site for barely an hour," Ferguson said, "and we haven't found much yet."

Jason said, "The drones that attacked us . . . They self-destructed. You guys find any of the wreckage yet?"

"Bits and pieces. The only remnants that are still mostly intact are the rifles that were attached. They're M4 Carbines. No serial numbers, of course. But we'll work to try and figure out where they came from."

"Is everyone inside the facility all right?"

Ferguson nodded. "The site went on lockdown following the attack. No one was able to get out."

"That's not right," Jason said. "They should've been able to come out and help."

The agent shrugged. "I don't know how things work here. Didn't even know this place existed until an hour ago."

Jason stowed the information, then said, "What about Marcus?" When the agent looked confused, he added, "Retired Brigadier General Marcus Chapman. Decorated Green Beret and the head of this facility. He was shot by the drones, and his body washed down the river. He needs to be found and given a proper burial."

Ferguson slid out his phone and placed a call.

"He would've entered the river two hours and forty-five minutes ago, if it helps locate him."

Jason and Alejandra stepped away from the agent and stared at the barely noticeable exterior of the facility.

"I knew someone must've hacked into the system, but this . . ." Jason shook his head. "This is another level."

Someone had gone to great lengths to have him killed. But who and why?

Agent Ferguson ended the call, and then his phone rang again. He spoke for ten seconds, then cupped the phone to his shoulder. "We've found the launch site for the drones. It's five miles north of here."

THIRTEEN

JASON, ALEJANDRA, AND Agent Ferguson climbed into the helicopter and flew the five miles north. They landed on a desolate scraggly expanse of land between the edge of a cliff and a steady slope filled with massive boulders. There were no roads or signs of human life, aside from charred wreckage that looked like a mini crater.

They hopped out when the skids touched down, rushed away from the rotor's slipstream, and went straight for the wreckage. Jason stopped beside the blackened remains of a wheel, a melted tire, and pieces of paneling and grooved flat sections.

"Looks like a flatbed," Jason said.

Alejandra nodded. "What's with these guys and blowing their stuff up?"

Jason kneeled and inspected the debris. "Covering their tracks."

As the other two combed the area, Jason climbed onto a pyramid-shaped rock that drove twenty feet into the sky. He stopped at the apex and looked around. The sun was arcing overhead, and the temperature was flirting with three figures, despite it not being noon yet. The landscape baked and boiled all around him.

Jason gazed off to the south, tracing an imaginary line to where he thought Tenth Circle was. Then he looked to the north, where the vehicle must've driven in from. He'd have to consult a map, but he figured there had to be a dirt road within half a mile of their position.

He ran through the attack. There'd been three vehicles in all: the drone launch truck, whatever the guys in the ghillie suits had been driving, and the backup team in the Escalade. They must've dropped off the drone launch truck and let it sit concealed in the middle of nowhere, waiting for the opportune moment to strike. Three drones soaring and zipping across the sky. A surprise attack. Then the truck self-destructs, and eventually, so do all three of the drones so as not to leave any trace.

He eyed the remaining wreckage.

Well, leave little to no trace.

Jason thought of the guys who'd been hunting him.

"Roadblocks catch anyone suspicious?" he said to Agent Ferguson.

The man kept his eyes down, sifting through the remnants of the truck. "No one yet."

And they weren't likely to. Though the sniper had missed him, he'd *barely* missed him with near hits from over five hundred yards away on a moving target and tall sporadic brush to contend with. The guys in the ghillie suits were professionals. Expert assassins. Notches above the guys he'd encountered at the gas station. And those guys hadn't exactly been amateurs.

By then, the guys in the ghillie suits would probably be in Mexico, or wherever the hell they wanted to be. Maybe standing by at a discreet motel, formulating a new strategy to engage him, and backed by guys with a whole lot of money and know-how and access to advanced drones.

Jason climbed back down and headed for the helicopter.

"You gonna help us?" Ferguson said.

"We're not gonna find anything."

Ferguson's phone rang. He answered, then his eyes lit up, and he held the device out in front of him.

"What is it?" Alejandra said, she and Jason closing in.

He twisted his hand and aimed the screen toward them as they approached. It was a clear picture of one of the drones soaring in a blue sky.

"Apparently, one of Tenth Circle's security cameras caught this," he said.

"I thought the system was hacked?" Jason said.

The agent shrugged. "Apparently, not the whole system."

Ferguson typed quick messages while asking questions to the agent who'd called him.

"Were you able to recover anything else from the security feeds?" Jason asked.

"That's it," the agent replied. "Just glimpses from that camera. Everything else was hacked, and the hard drives were erased."

"It looks like a quadcopter," Alejandra said.

Jason said, "It was, and they were big. Though I never got a great look at them. It was bright, and they were fast and far off. They had good range and flight time, which is impressive for a craft weighed down by an automatic rifle and so much ammunition."

Ferguson forwarded the image to Jason, who sent it to Elliot "Murph" Murphy, a renowned hacker and brilliant inventor who he and his team had worked with on multiple operations.

"It's a multi-purpose military drone," Ferguson said, receiving word from analysts just minutes after getting the image. "Designed in Iran for use by their Revolutionary Guard Corps."

FOURTEEN

AT THAT SAME moment, two thousand miles away, a Dassault Falcon 50 super-midsize jet taxied onto the tarmac at the Great Inagua Coast Guard Base in The Bahamas. The aircraft was given an immediate green light on the quiet runway and blasted off the apron.

CIA Special Agent Kate Royal sat in the nearly empty private cabin. Beside her was her longtime partner, Jake Nielson, and across from them sat three men, all of them handcuffed and locked to their seats with hoods over their heads.

The order had been given thirty minutes prior, and it had come from the top. Given recent events and the tensions they'd caused, the executive decision had been made to move the three witnesses Stateside. After their cargo vessel was boarded by a joint team of Navy and Coast Guard servicemen, the crew had been airlifted to the remote Coast Guard base, where they'd been confined and questioned ever since. None of them had spoken a word, but now the three foreigners were being taken to a witness holding and interrogation facility under the FBI's main Division office in Miami to be questioned by a team of expert interrogators—the kind of people who can make anyone crack.

The original plan was for the three to be taken to the nearest military holding installation: Guantanamo Bay on Cuba's southeastern coast. But that idea was thrown out after the cargo ship's logs had been checked and cross-referenced with those at the shipping port in Havana—the last place the vessel docked before setting sail just twelve hours before the missile was fired.

The recent events had put the US in a difficult position, as neither country had the cleanest track record with the States, and the connection had forced the Joint Chiefs to take every possibility into account. And so the decision was made to instead bring the witnesses to the mainland, where they could be held and interrogated properly. Their testimonies, if acquired, could be used in talks with the Iranian government.

The flight took just shy of an hour, and Agent Royal spent every second of it watching the prisoners, wishing she could read their minds. Having spent nine years with the Agency, the tough, pretty, five foot two blond force of nature was no stranger to high-risk, classified details. She was a fast riser, an all-star who excelled, no matter the task. And her supervisors had taken notice. Dedicated and highly intelligent, she'd quickly made a name for herself as one of the best agents in the organization.

Royal and her partner had been in Florida investigating a new method of arms trafficking when they received the unexpected call. The mission to handle the transport of the three prisoners was an important test in their careers, but Royal had more reason than just her career to be invested in the mission. A quick scan of the classified report informed her that the missile attack was linked to a past incident that could potentially lead to tracking down a killer she'd been hunting for five long years. The mission was personal for her. A vendetta. Not that anyone in the Agency knew about it except for the man beside her, but he never said a word and always had her back.

The wheels touched down at Fort Lauderdale-Hollywood International Airport, and the craft wheeled to a stop in a private corner of the runway, where three bulletproof SUVs, two police cars, and four motorcycles were parked.

Royal and Nielson unlocked the three men and ushered them to the door, out into the midday heat, and down the steps. Men in suits and sunglasses met them at the vehicles. The doors to the back SUV were opened, and the three prisoners were helped inside. Nielson sat in the back seat, right behind the prisoners. Royal sat angled in the passenger seat so she could maintain her stare at the three captives.

Without a word, the driver fired up the engine. The police vehicles powered on their lights and sirens, and the motorcade cruised off the apron in a line. Driving straight through the inner security checkpoint, they cut across a lot and past a guard shack and open gate, the two armed guards staring as the commotion rushed by.

Royal scanned the road ahead of them. It was just after lunchtime, which meant busy, crowded streets. But the lights and sirens paved the way for them, the lines of cars parting and gravitating to the shoulders to give them a nice spread of empty pavement. The motorcade maintained speed well over the limit as it raced inland. They didn't have far to go—barely twenty miles, which they could make in fifteen minutes at their current speed.

Royal's gaze formed a triangle, going from the prisoners behind her, to the road ahead, to her watch. The trip was going as expected until halfway to their destination, when they saw a tower of steam shooting out from the road ahead of them. A manhole was open, and a team of construction workers were on scene, blocking the road as they fought to control the release of heated vapor.

"I thought the route was clear," Royal said into her radio, communicating with an FBI helicopter observing their position.

"It was a minute ago," a voice replied.

Royal thought for a second. "All units, redirect. We're taking the alternate route."

Royal didn't like it. She didn't believe in coincidences.

The motorcade snaked left at the intersection, veering past the workers and the pillar of steam. They drove on for three minutes, then rushed through an intersection and passed a parking garage that ran for an entire block near the back of a shopping center.

Three quarters of the way down the block, sudden, rapid-fire shots rang out.

Two shooters were opening fire from the second-level parking garage, sparking rounds off the bulletproof SUVs. The motorcade took evasive action, accelerating faster and splitting up at the next intersection. Royal's SUV turned right, screeching around the turn and flying toward a line of packing facilities and warehouses lining a reservoir. One squad car followed right behind them, and two police motorcycles took the lead.

Royal clicked her seatbelt and cursed. She pictured their position in her mind, along with the escort plan she'd cooked up, and made the decision to change the plan again.

"We're heading to Pembroke Pines instead," Royal said to the driver and into the radio.

The police station was less than a mile from their current position and served as one of the backup destinations in what her superiors dubbed the "unlikely event" of an ambush. While the FBI building was still six miles away, they could make the station in under two minutes.

"What the hell," the driver said, easing off the gas and onto the brake.

He kept his eyes forward as the two motorcycles braked to a complete stop ahead of them. Forced to stop as well, the driver looked left and right, and then down. Agent Royal leaned forward and peered down at a glistening object strung out across the street. It was a spike strip—the same device used by law enforcement to stop wheeled vehicles by puncturing their tires.

The moment Royal realized what it was, in her peripheral, she saw a big yellow blur flying straight toward them. She turned her head just in time to see a school bus roaring down the steep gradient of an alley. The driver saw it too, his eyes bulging and his foot instinctively racing for the gas pedal. He managed to depress it and screech the big vehicle forward, but it was a fraction of a second too late.

The bus rammed into the back of the SUV, jerking the vehicle into a violent spin before flipping over. The sudden ear-piercing impact jarred the occupants of the vehicle in a chaotic blur of extreme force. It threw Royal into the dashboard, then back against her door like a rag doll. Her ears rang, and her consciousness faded as the world blurred around her. There was nothing but noise and flashes of light, and then the SUV completed its rotation and crashed into the rail, breaking free and soaring five feet down before splashing into the edge of the reservoir.

Water sprayed away from the cratered vehicle, swallowing it and turning the world cold. The chaos of the collision immediately gave way to gushing water bursting into the space.

Royal was delirious and her vision hazy. Her body throbbed, and adrenaline jolted her senses. She flashed back into consciousness when the cold water rushed up over her legs and chest. The driver was motionless, the water rising over his bloodied head.

The water kissed her chin, and she knew she had seconds, nothing more. The air was bubbling out rapidly, water taking its place. She looked back. Two of the prisoners were unconscious, and the third cried out and struggled to break free of his restraints. Behind them, Agent Nielson was alive but fighting the same battle with pain and confusion that she was.

He seemed to blink to reality also with the cold of the reservoir and climbed forward. The water was racing toward the roof. Royal unclipped her seat belt, ignoring the blood dripping down her face. Nielsen had his keys out and was fighting to free the stuck prisoner.

"It wasn't us. It wasn't us!" the terrified captive shouted as death knocked on his doorstep.

With inches of dry space left, she and Nielson sucked in a final breath.

The SUV filled with water and sank rapidly, dropping toward the bottom like a stone. It struck grime, and Royal could barely see anything, but she felt the pressure change, and her ears adjusted and popped once. In her experience, that meant they were roughly ten feet down.

She reached to help her partner but could barely see a couple inches in front of her face. A figure appeared on the opposite side of the vehicle. At first, Royal thought it was one of the officers swimming down, but she quickly realized it was a diver. The mysterious person held out a speargun and launched the sharp projectile through Nielson's throat, murdering Royal's partner right before her eyes. Before she could attempt a retaliation, the diver finned closer and buried a knife into the neck of the struggling prisoner. Royal twisted and withdrew her pistol as the cold-blooded killer viciously finished off the other two prisoners with his knife.

Royal kept herself steady from the passenger seat and took aim with her Glock 19. She knew it could fire at least a couple shots underwater because she'd done it before, but the friction of the water would quickly slow the round, so she'd need to hit her target from near point-blank range.

She reached her gun hand forward as far as it would go. Just as the diver realized she was there, she pulled the trigger, causing a muffled boom, a brief flash, and a discharge of bubbles. The bullet launched out of the barrel like a torpedo and struck the man. She fired again and again, managing three shots before her weapon seized up. The diver jolted back, and she released her weapon and pushed herself backward, shoving her already cracked door the rest of the way open.

Her lungs were screaming, her heart pounding. She forced herself out, breaking free of the underwater coffin. Not knowing if there were more divers, she kicked with everything she had and tore at the water with cupped hands, her gaze locked skyward.

Royal broke free, sucking in a deep lungful of air as the brightness and noise and heat overwhelmed her. She took in two more breaths while scanning the surface, then swam for the shore. Three police officers stood above her, barking words she couldn't understand over the ringing in her ears.

FIFTEEN

SPECIAL AGENT KATE Royal had barely caught her breath when she lost it again. A faint sloshing of water caught her attention at the reservoir's edge, then a thrashing body rose out from the murk. A man wearing a black wetsuit and rebreather climbed onto the muddy shore. His fins were already gone, and she watched him for a moment as he struggled with straps and tore off the rest of his gear. He tossed his mask and was about to peel off his wetsuit when he saw her.

Still dazed, but with adrenaline rushing through her and anger taking hold, she whistled to the nearby officers, pointed toward the diver, and yelled that the attacker was there. Then she dove headlong back into the water.

She went right into a ferocious freestyle, her powerful strokes allowing her to cut the distance to the muddy bank in under a minute. She heaved herself out and splashed onto the shore just as the diver stumbled up to a path and scurried into the shadows behind a wall. He was hurt, limping slightly, and had an arm pressed to his chest.

Royal dashed up the muddy slope and heaved herself onto the path. Soaked and tired and dazed, she pushed through, running with everything she had to catch up to the shooter.

Her head pounded, and her soaked clothes made running difficult, but the guy she pursued was wearing a thick, skintight wetsuit, restricting his movements. And she knew if he didn't get medical attention soon for his gunshots, he'd be done for.

The diver cut into a big warehouse, shouldering through a door that flew open and smacked against the inner wall. She closed in, following him into the dark doorway, and entering thirty seconds after her quarry.

The bright sky shone at her back, giving way to the shadows inside the abandoned warehouse. She expected to see the diver halfway across the room, stumbling and making a last-ditch effort to escape. She imagined she'd spring over and hunt him down like a lioness on the plains. But there was no sign of him.

With the surrounding darkness and stacks of crates providing cover, and with no glimpse of the killer, she felt suddenly vulnerable. But the fog was lifting, the sudden rush of oxygen to her brain from exercise giving clarity. She patted her empty holster and remembered she was unarmed, then bent down and grabbed her backup weapon—a subcompact Glock 43 offering seven 9mm rounds—holstered to her ankle.

She passed a line of dust-coated crates, scanning the space with her eyes and weapon. Sirens grew louder outside, and backup was moving in. The guy couldn't hide out in there forever. She thought about backstepping out and making sure he didn't leave, but that wasn't her way. It'd never been her way.

From the opposite corner, the sharp ringing of a bolt colliding and tumbling on the concrete floor caught her attention. The guy was still there—she was sure of that. The warehouse had three other doors. Two were locked with chains, and the third had a hefty handle caked with rust and looked like it hadn't been operated in ten years. If he'd used it, she would've heard it.

She closed in on the sound, her pistol raised, her eyes and ears alert. The corner was dark, but a faint beam of light glaring through a faded window illuminated a bolt resting on the floor. Beside it was a tall shelf.

As she moved in, footsteps resounded from behind her. She turned as the diver popped out from behind a crate and charged, clasping a four-foot steel pipe. Royal fired twice in rapid succession. The rounds struck him in the chest, puncturing the wetsuit and causing him to grunt and jolt, but not stopping him.

Before she could fire a third, the guy shouted and swung the pipe, bashing it into Royal's hip. She leaned with the blow, just like they'd been taught in training, but the force was severe, nearly breaking bone and shooting pain up her body.

The big man kicked her to the ground and reared overhead for another strike. Royal rolled, barely escaping the whooshing pipe as it whipped down and smacked against the concrete, vibrating and ringing from the force. Royal scrambled behind a crate, and the injured diver grunted and quickly shoved it aside. She crawled back as he swung again, striking the floor and missing her left leg by mere inches.

As he reared back for a strike to her head, she faked left, then caught him off guard by rolling back toward him. Royal took aim and fired in a blink. The bullet burst into the base of his neck, and he shook as he dropped the pipe and collapsed like a marionette with the strings cut.

She got up and staggered over to the downed man.

"Shit," she whispered, then knelt beside him and felt for a pulse.

SIXTEEN

JASON AND ALEJANDRA made the two-hundred-mile jump from the truck's wreckage site to Laughlin Air Force Base. Alejandra had wanted to skip across the country and back to The Bahamas as quickly as possible, so she flew in their operation's newest aircraft.

They climbed aboard a Lockheed Martin supersonic jet that was capable of reaching speeds up to Mach 2.2, or nearly seventeen hundred miles per hour, making it one of the fastest aircraft in the world. The blazing marvel of aviation technology was still technically in its developmental stages, but Jason's financial situation opened a lot of doors and allowed the team to access technologies not available to the general public. A substantial investment in the aircraft's project six months earlier allowed them to receive one of the first prototypes for their private use.

The two operatives settled into the sleek, comfortable cabin, and were wheels up in five minutes, ascending to a cruising altitude of sixty thousand feet and blasting through the stratosphere at over twice the speed of sound.

Jason used the brief moment of downtime to message one of their operation's financial specialists. He pictured Tuck Jackson, the weathered, blue-collar Texan who'd saved his life and was about to get a substantial monetary surprise.

They'd been airborne barely ten minutes when Jason's sat phone rang. It was Murph finally getting back to him. It seemed that with every passing minute, they had more questions than answers, and Murph was their go-to guy for answers.

"What have you got, Murph?" Jason said.

"It looks like an Iranian drone, all right. The contours of the arms are the dead giveaway, along with the relatively spartan central assembly. Like the FBI concluded, it was one of the many multi-purpose combat drones developed for Iran's Revolutionary Guard. Far as I can tell, it was intended mostly for surveillance, but it's capable of carrying a payload up to thirty pounds. Based on the photographs, the rifle appears to be a partially disassembled M4 Carbine, like you said. Rather genius, really."

"Looks like something a high schooler could weld up in a shop class," Alejandra chimed in.

"Exactly," Murph said. "The simplicity is what's so genius about it. It would've been a hell of a lot harder to smuggle fully functional military drones into the country with firepower intact, so these guys made a smart move. They just smuggled the drones in. Nothing unusual about that. No visible threat. The thing looks like a lot of commercial drones, just bigger. Then they get them into the States, and all they need to do is buy weapons at any of the million or so gun shops in Texas. Then they just disassemble them, and there they have it. Three effective, long-range attack drones with surplus ammunition, provided by drum magazines. Ready to deploy."

"And with self-destruct capabilities," Jason said.

"Yeah . . . still trying to fully figure that one out. Must've been trying to hide something. There's info stored in the CPUs of those advanced units. You're sure they self-destructed?"

"Positive."

"All right. I'll keep that in mind."

Jason pinched the bridge of his nose. "What about the hacking of Tenth Circle's systems?"

"I just got the info, and I'm running over it now. It's too early to formulate anything other than that it's an impressive accomplishment. Their systems were good. I know that because I helped design them. But I don't want to give my take until I've been through it all and have a solid conclusion as to what happened."

"Well, Murph, I'll let you get back to it." Jason remembered the brief discussion with the hitman in the back of the gas station. "Quick, before you go. Does the name Cipher happen to mean anything to you?"

Murph fell silent a moment, then his voice came back slower. "Where did you hear that name?"

"One of the guys who'd been trying to kill me said it right before he dug a cyanide tablet from the corner of his mouth and chomped on it. He said Cipher was the one hunting me down."

"Well, that changes things," Murph said, his tone taking a grave turn. "That changes . . . everything."

SEVENTEEN

THE JET TOUCHED down at Chub Cay Airport in the Berry Islands less than an hour after taking off from Texas, and Jason and Alejandra switched into a helicopter for the short remainder of the journey.

It was 1400 local time when the R/V *Valiant* came into view, anchored off the northern coast of the unpopulated Bonds Cay along the eastern edge of the Bahamian island chain. The 200-foot research vessel wasn't much to look at. By outward appearance, she was an ordinary and slightly rundown research vessel—a bit on the small side and aged, with rust at the seams. She had a faded dark blue hull, a white superstructure, and featured a big deck crane and A-frame winches. Even the helipad was usually discreetly stowed, the platform folding out on the bow and giving the pilots ample landing room as they approached.

The waters below were perfect, pristine and untouched. A true paradise. One look at the water sparked a flicker of primal excitement within Jason's mind, and he felt like it'd been an eternity since he was in the tropics. Not since his time in the Azores, though that'd only been for a few hours before he'd rushed away to New York City.

On approach, Jason ran his eyes over long stretches of bleached sand and lapping surf, shorelines frosted with turquoise waters, and specks of land covered in rich greens.

But he wasn't there to soak in the paradise before him. His gaze turned to the dark blue waters of the Tongue of the Ocean, and the near-instant transition to shallows and corals, the underwater ledges right beside the *Valiant*.

He took in the wide, blue horizon. Somewhere out there were the remnants of a missile launch site—clues that needed to be found and evaluated. He could feel the clock ticking. Though the threat of assassins hunting him down was strong, Jason knew that tensions between the US and Iran were at an all-time high. If they didn't draw some strong conclusions quickly, war would be imminent. That much was certain.

They touched down on the helipad, and Jason and Alejandra jumped out. Scott met them on the bow, the athletic, middle-aged leader of their covert group all seriousness as he ushered them away from the wind and sounds of the rotor.

They slipped inside through a watertight door, and Scott shut it behind them. "Good to see you," he said, patting Jason on the shoulder.

Jason could see that he was saying a lot more. He was glad Jason had made it out, glad he'd somehow managed to survive the ordeal, and he was sorry to hear about Marcus. Scott and the distinguished Green Beret had gone back over twenty years. He could see the anguish deep in Scott's eyes, but the trained military and political professional was good at keeping those emotions at bay—those understandable human reactions to tragedy—because men in his position had no choice. The objective always came first. There was no point in breaking down and wallowing and cursing the fates. Not then, at least. There was a mission at hand.

"Maintain your focus on the task before you," as Marcus would say.

He also would've told them not to let his death be in vain.

They speed-walked up to the bridge. Once there, Jason gazed out over the water and glanced at the rows of monitors displaying various images and data.

"Heard from Murph?" Scott said.

"Just his info on the drones from the attack on Tenth Circle. They were Iranian."

"I heard."

"But he's analyzing the data from the facility's security breach now. He also might be able to give us info on who orchestrated the attack in Texas."

That got all of Scott's attention, and Jason added, "One of the hitmen gave up a name. Cipher. That's all I know at this point, and when I told Murph, he got jittery and anxious and had to end the call right away and get to work."

Scott nodded. "The name must mean something to him. Hopefully, it leads somewhere. I also have him looking into the origins of this cruise missile."

"Keeping him busy. How's the search?"

Finn appeared, striding into the room with a tablet. This was usually the part where he and Jason exchanged joking, fun-loving jabs, but that wasn't going to happen. Not that day.

He just gave Jason and Alejandra a knowing nod. "Glad you both made it," he said.

"I was just about to give them an update on the search," Scott said.

He led them over to the monitors. One of them displayed a GPS image of the *Valiant* and its surroundings. He zoomed out by tapping the screen, then pressed a button to display a green track of the *Valiant*'s position over the past couple of hours.

"We started here, where the missile was first spotted on radar," Scott said. "Then we ran a wide sweep with the sonar. Not easy. The water's deep. The going was slow. We followed the entire path that the Iranian cargo ship had taken prior to it being intercepted by the Guard."

"Following orders from up top," Finn chimed in.

"I'm guessing you didn't find anything?" Alejandra said.

Scott shook his head. "Nothing that could be a launch site. And every inch of the container ship was searched. There was no sign of any launch systems there, either."

Jason analyzed the map a moment. "Looks like we're back near where the missile was first spotted on radar."

"Correct," Scott said. "Finn has a theory."

All eyes went to the sharp, educated Latino. "It's far-fetched, I know," he said. "But prior to all this going down, we were on our way here. Well, we were on our way nearby, to Chub Cay, to meet with a dive shop owner. That's why we were hailed to search for the blown-up missile. We were cruising up the Strait and were less than fifty miles from where it was shot out of the sky."

"Why were you meeting with the shop owner?" Jason asked.

"That's the thing. We were on our way here to investigate six people who died—a group of tourists and the two dive operators. All of them washed ashore on Whale Key, and their dive boat still hasn't been found. It happened a week ago, and the whole thing was written up like it was probably an accident, but it didn't seem right to me. I've been taking out dive charters in Los Roques for years and doing dives all over long before that. The whole thing was off, and we'd already been in the Gulf of Mexico following an incident involving a secret underwater arsenal, so we motored here right after to investigate."

"What's your theory?" Jason said.

He took a moment to collect his thoughts. "What if those six people were murdered because they found something? Something that someone powerful didn't want them to?"

Jason nearly smiled but kept it back as he peered out through the big windows. His team had been carefully chosen by him and Scott, and each for good reason. They were a group of highly intelligent and focused individuals, and each had an intuition X factor that proved the key to their operations success, time and time again.

"How long ago did you wrap up this search pattern?" Jason said. He pointed at a green line on the monitor running across the TOTO, to where the container ship had been seized, along with another line back down to their current position.

"We just got back," Scott said. "The submersible's being prepped and lowered as we speak."

Scott leaned closer to a different monitor that displayed the immediate water surrounding them, showing depths and underwater formations.

"We'll run cross patterns with the *Valiant* here," he said, running his finger over the deep water. "Mow the lawn in a nice, wide search radius around the spot where the missile was first picked up. It was flying at over six hundred miles per hour, so even a two-second delay in its initial spotting would've resulted in a substantial error in its predicted launch location. If we don't find anything with that, we'll widen it even more."

"And I'll be piloting the sub here," Finn said. "The water's shallower along the ledge and then gets even shallower as it angles up to the outer portions of the reef systems."

"Alejandra and I could be in the water here," Jason said, pointing to an area that averaged just sixty feet deep. "We could dive down with the sea scooters and handheld magnetometers."

Scott nodded. "If something's there, we'll find it."

EIGHTEEN

JASON DROPPED BACKWARD, flipping over the side of the RHIB and splashing into paradise in full scuba gear. The warm water covered him and swirled in a bubbly vortex for half a second before clearing and allowing him to see the edge of the shelf and sprawling reefs. The area was strictly protected, so the reefs were lively and colorful and healthy.

Entering negatively buoyant, he sank ten feet, then leveled off and looked around. The current was slow at maybe a quarter of a knot, and the viz was about as good as it gets anywhere on Earth, allowing him to see nearly a hundred feet.

Jason could hear the distant pings of the submersible's active sonar, the little bleeps sounding off rhythmically. The sound waves bounced off the seafloor and returned to the sub at different intervals, allowing the computer to create a digital replication of the seafloor. Members of the crew still aboard the *Valiant* surveyed the sonar readings and would provide backup, letting Finn know if they spotted anything unusual. Meanwhile, Scott was on the bridge, the *Valiant* making slow sweeps along the outer shelf and working its way out into the deeper waters of the TOTO.

Alejandra splashed down from the other side of the boat right after Jason, sinking down and leveling her buoyancy right beside him. They both held brand-new sea scooters, the advanced little devices capable of pulling them through the water at up to seven miles per hour. And the team's latest version had an improved battery life, giving them forty-five minutes at full speed. They also had two more fully charged batteries still on the RHIB to prolong their search, if need be.

Jason and Alejandra split up, him heading north and her south along the same line. They agreed to cover a hundred yards before moving west to a new line and motoring back. Aside from the scuba gear and scooters, they had full facemasks and radios so they could communicate with each other, Finn, and the *Valiant*. They also had portable magnetometers set with wide swaths. The devices were nice to have, but they were mainly relying on their eyes. They all knew that whatever had been used as a base to launch the missile shouldn't be difficult to spot from close-up with the naked eye.

Jason held on tight as the device rapidly torpedoed him up to its max speed. He eased back, wanting to give each area a thorough sweep before moving on, and after peering up over the underwater landscape, the task seemed daunting. The reefs appeared to never end and rose up and down in thick clusters of various species of coral and marine life bunched tightly together—all intermixed into an intricate series of unique, jutting rock formations.

Five minutes in, he spotted a hammerhead cruising along the shallow ledge. The two made eye contact, then it swam closer a moment before confidently wandering out to deeper water.

He saw nothing unusual as he wrapped up the first pass, no sign that man had ever been there at all, aside from a few beer cans and plastic bottles.

Jason turned and held on, motoring ten yards west before cutting back in the direction he'd come. "Anyone pick up anything yet?" he said into his radio.

In turn, Alejandra, Finn, and Scott all replied in the negative.

He completed the sweep nearly at the same time as Alejandra, the athletic Latina beating him by a few seconds.

"Let's switch for the second lap," Jason said.

She agreed and took off, racing north while Jason headed south, keeping his eyes peeled.

The underwater world was beautiful, a magnificent paradise teeming with life, and Jason spotted an abundance of angel fish, grouper, various parrotfish, and a school of glistening bonefish. But he saw nothing unusual—no sign of anything metal, and the handheld magnetometer hadn't made a peep.

He reached the end, then cut back again and met up with Alejandra once more. The two repeated the search pattern for three more laps and didn't find anything. Jason checked his dive watch. They'd been down for thirty minutes, swept over half an acre of seafloor, and had come up empty.

Jason called in to the others again and got the same quick reply. No one had spotted anything remotely unusual in the untouched paradise, and given that they'd swept the entire search area, there appeared to be nothing down there.

Jason looked toward the outer edges of the search area and thought about what Scott had said about the missile's speed and how easily it could be somewhere outside where they expected it to be. He reasoned that they could be searching for a very long time and wondered if it was still the viable approach.

He scanned a full three-sixty turn, then stared to the west where the water shallowed even more. The bottom arched steadily toward the surface for about a football field, then plateaued again at roughly forty feet deep. The coral heads and rock formations were even bigger there, some sprouting up close to the surface. And there were crevices dropping deep and winding along the seafloor, packed with color and life.

Jason was just about to mention that they should try a different approach—that they should go back to the drawing board and make sure they found the correct search area. Maybe double- and triple-check the coordinates. Or maybe even question whether the radar could've been off, or late reacting, to the point of being near useless, giving a real search area that would take weeks to scour.

But the thoughts slipped from his mind when he saw a flash, a glimmer of late-afternoon light shining back at him. At first, he thought it was a fish—a wayward bonefish or a silver spade. But then the light flashed again, coming from the same spot, and he angled his head and realized it was his movements that were causing the light to flash in and out of view.

"What is it?" Alejandra said, seeing him stare toward the shallower water.

"I don't know," Jason replied, adjusting his position and firing up his sea scooter.

He held on, rocketed fifty yards across the underwater world, and descended toward the glimmer.

Probably nothing, he thought. *Probably just a piece of trash. A shard of a glass bottle or busted-up aluminum can.*

But it wasn't either of those things.

He powered down the propeller and grabbed hold of a rock to steady himself as he angled his mask for a closer look at the shiny object. It had jagged edges but was smooth on both its flat sides. A portion of its backside was exposed and painted black.

Jason adjusted his body and grabbed it so he could examine the credit-card-sized object more thoroughly. The non-painted side was metal, unpolished, but smooth.

Alejandra motored up and stopped right behind him. Before she could ask what he'd found, Jason turned and held out the shard. She cocked her head as she took it from him and inspected it.

"Initial thoughts?" Jason said.

"I was about to ask you the same thing."

She handed the shard back to Jason, and he pocketed it.

"You guys find something?" Scott's voice said through the tiny speaker.

"Maybe, maybe not," Jason said.

He did another 360-degree sweep of the seafloor around him. It was unique, full of fascinating rock formations, like pillars sprouting up all around them.

"Let's split again here," Jason said. "Do some circular sweeps starting at this spot and see what we can find."

They descended to just five feet above the coral-coated bottom and rounded away from each other while arcing slowly to the west. After completing the quick search, they managed to find more similar, various-shaped shards, but that was it. They cut back and descended into the crevices, switching on dive lights and peeking into every nook and cranny in the reef system. They both spotted more shards, but nothing bigger than the first one. Soon, they were back where they started.

"I don't get it," Jason said, looking around. "What are these things, and where did they come from?"

Alejandra didn't answer. She just scanned around them more and shined her light into the maze of tight spaces below.

Scott's voice came through the speaker. "We've finished our sweep. We found nothing."

"Me, neither," Finn chimed in.

Jason said, "Give us a couple more minutes, Scott. I feel like we might be close to something."

They split off again, searching deeper into the spaces and widening their search radius from the first shard they'd found.

After another ten minutes passed with nothing to show for it, Jason sighed a trail of bubbles, then checked his pressure gauge. "I've got seven hundred pounds left, Ali. Let's head back up to the RHIB."

He watched Alejandra fin over grooves in the seafloor and was about to hail her again when she froze, then kicked, descending rapidly out of his view.

"What do we have here?" she said, a hint of excitement in her voice.

Jason kicked in big, powerful cycles, closing the distance between him and the last place he'd seen her. He barely spotted her in the darkness below and angled his body down, following right behind her and weaving through wide branches of fan coral.

The water darkened as they descended twenty feet toward the bottom. Alejandra aimed her flashlight into a clearing, and they both gasped.

NINETEEN

THEIR FLASHLIGHTS SHONE over long metal sheets, broken apart and spread out along the flat underbelly of the crevice beneath them. Intermixed were more shards, some bigger than the first ones they'd found. From the surface, camouflaged by coral and the natural contours of the seafloor and shrouded in shadows, the remnants would've been impossible to spot.

They vented air from their BCDs and descended closer. Checking his dive computer, Jason saw that they were back to sixty feet down. The sheets of metal were thick, and upon closer inspection, they could see that it was formed into grooves. The objects took form in their minds nearly at the same time.

Alejandra said, "This was a shipping container."

It became clear. They were floating over the remains of a shipping container that Jason reasoned had been twenty feet long and lowered vertically into the opening of rock. And then, eventually, it'd been blown to pieces.

Scott's voice returned in the speaker. "You guys find something?"

Jason clicked on his bodycam, aimed the lens at the wreckage, and shined his light.

"Oh, yeah," he said. "We found something."

Jason closed in on one of the container's walls and saw something unusual on the white-painted letters set against the dark blue backdrop. He removed one of his gloves and ran his bare hand over the outside of the sheet. After pulling his hand back, he rubbed the thin layer of algae on his fingertips together to form a small cloud of marine growth. The trails he'd made along the exterior of the sheet weren't much—like a fish tank that hadn't been scrubbed for a week, but they exposed a powerful revelation, nonetheless.

"Safe to say your theory was right, Finn," Jason said into the radio. "This structure's been down here for weeks."

While sifting through the heart of the wreckage, Jason and Alejandra found broken and burned pieces of circuit boards and intricate wiring, along with more smooth metal shards.

"Those look like pieces of an air compressor chamber," Finn's voice said through the speaker.

"For controlling the buoyancy while lowering the container into position?" Alejandra said.

"For firing the missile," Finn said. "In order to be launched beneath the surface, an initial blast of pressurized air would've been needed to torpedo the missile up out of the water. Then once it broke free, its engines kicked in, rocketing it into the air."

"That fully kills the theory that it was fired from the Iranian ship," Jason said. "Not that a vessel with that kind of draft would be able to maneuver over this spot anyway."

They spent five minutes inspecting and filming the scene. Jason felt a faint sense of déjà vu as he surveyed the wreckage. It reminded him of hours earlier when he was back in the Texas desert, combing the scattered remains of the truck that had been used to launch the attack drones.

The launch of the missile hadn't caused the container to blow apart, which meant there'd been a charge in place—one set to blow away the launch site after the missile had already been fired, cleaning up the scene a little bit. The sea had already dispersed much of the remains, the currents scattering and burying parts of the wreckage. In a month, most of the pieces would be spread out and buried. And in a year, the sea would take over, and there'd be little that wasn't covered in marine life.

Not that it matters much, Jason thought as he looked toward the surface.

The encroaching coral and rock formations made the thing nearly impossible to find unless you knew it was there.

Jason thought back to the divers Finn had mentioned—the tourists who, along with the dive operators, had mysteriously died. He figured that somehow they'd managed to find the container before the missile launch and that somehow, whoever was hiding it, managed to see them do it and take action.

"But if the container was used to fire the missile while submerged," Alejandra said, "why had the Iranian cargo ship been there at all? What purpose did it serve?"

TWENTY

JASON AND ALEJANDRA returned to the RHIB, fired up its twin Mercury 150-horsepower engines, and flew back to the *Valiant*. A door hinged up at the stern, and Alejandra eased off the throttle before piloting them straight toward it. The fiberglass hull made contact with a rubber conveyor belt that grabbed hold of their craft and pulled them out of the water. In a smooth, quick process, the belt brought them into the RHIB deployment room.

Just as the boat cleared the discreet entryway, hydraulics kicked in, and the door glided back down and locked into place. They grabbed their gear and heaved it forward through a watertight door, down a short set of stairs, and into the central deployment room, or "rec room."

The top of the moonpool was open, and bubbles were rumbling up from the water. The submersible appeared seconds after they stepped inside, and after handing their gear to one of the group's dive technicians, they helped hook a compact crane to the top of the sub and hoist it out of the water.

Finn opened the top hatch as it was raised, then climbed out and slid down, the wiry Venezuelan landing softly on the deck. "Scott just called," he said. "Apparently, shit's about to hit the fan."

As the words left his lips, the forward door opened and Scott appeared.

"Control room," he said. "Two minutes."

Jason and Alejandra peeled off their wetsuits, changed, and headed upstairs.

Scott and Finn were already in the control room when they arrived, and a fresh pot of coffee rested on a side table. Jason filled a mug. He wasn't a habitual coffee drinker, but after the day he had so far, he knew he needed the caffeine. He settled in at the table, and the group faced the monitor.

The screen brightened thirty seconds after they settled in, then an image appeared of an oblong rosewood table with a dozen decorated soldiers seated around it. The highest-ranking members of the United States armed forces faced each other, and at the head, President Elijah Martin sat leaned forward, his elbows resting on the table.

General Richardson, the chairman of the Joint Chiefs, spoke first. "The window for a decisive response is closing in on us. We've received warnings that if US troops advance any farther, Iranian ground units could begin targeting US transport vessels navigating the Strait of Hormuz. We've received intel regarding their military mobilizations along the coast, which puts us in a difficult spot."

"They're still denying any involvement with the missile attack?" Scott said.

"That's correct. They deny all knowledge of it. But more recent events have changed things. The crew members from the container ship are dead." He paused, letting the heavy statement settle. "They were killed in a well-organized and executed strike that took place outside of Miami just hours ago."

Jason and Scott exchanged glances.

"In addition to the crew members, two government agents were killed, and two local police officers were wounded."

"We know anything about the attackers?" Scott said.

The chairman nodded. "One of them was tracked down and killed by one of the CIA agents defending the ship's crew. There was a rushed identification process, and we just found out that the attacker was an Iranian mercenary." General Richardson scanned the room, then continued. "So, we have an Iranian missile fired from an Iranian container ship, then an Iranian mercenary taking down the only witnesses to the firing. Not to mention the incident at Chrome Canyon." He steepled his fingers. "But you say you found something?"

"Yes," Scott said. "We found the launch site. And the missile wasn't fired from the container ship."

The Joint Chiefs looked at each other quietly, then the president said, "Are you certain?"

"A hundred percent, Mr. President," Jason said. "The structure that was used to launch the missile has been resting on the seafloor for weeks."

Scott also explained how the launch site had been pressurized, indicating that the missile had been fired from underwater.

"It was Finn's theory," Jason said. "And he was right."

"What are you saying?" President Martin said.

Jason eyed the president. The two had met once before on a quiet evening in Capitol Hill Books in Washington, DC. But the middle-aged man looked different now, sitting straight and surrounded by the most powerful military leaders in the world. This was where big decisions were made, many of which had shaped the world over the past two hundred years.

"We believe someone is trying to frame Iran," Jason said, choosing his words carefully. "It's evident there's something deeper going on here beneath the surface.

Why would they fire the missile right when their own container ship was nearby if there was no reason for it to be there? And, General, you mentioned Chrome Canyon earlier. That attack wasn't on the training facility. They were trying to kill me. And why would Iran want to do that? It doesn't add up. The attack on Tenth Circle was ordered by someone who wants me dead. Somebody I've crossed before."

The president held out his hands. "Okay . . . who?"

Jason looked around the room. "We don't know. But it's the same person who tried to release the deadly virus on the world earlier this year. The one we barely stopped."

"General Kang and Zhao Song are both dead," the president said.

"They weren't the ones calling the shots," Scott said. "That person's still at large. And he's powerful."

President Martin said, "Okay . . . So, let's say for a second that you're right. What's the next step? Because right now, I've got a whole lot of evidence that paints Iran as the culprit, and I've got satellite footage of their troops mobilizing, and talks aren't exactly going well. We don't have a lot of time before a decision needs to be made."

"The next step would be figuring out who's really responsible, and then proving it," Scott said.

Jason stared intensely at the monitor. "We'll find the ones responsible, Mr. President. We just need time."

President Martin leaned back, tapping his index finger against his lip. He glanced at the men beside him, then shifted back forward. "You've got twenty-four hours. If you can't get me proof that Iran didn't perform the attacks by then, we'll have no choice but to cease all maritime traffic through the Strait of Hormuz and mobilize troops along their borders. This is as real as it gets, and any delay at a time like this, no matter how miniscule, can come back to haunt us down the road. Twenty-four hours is all I can spare. After that time elapses, we'll have no choice but to take preemptive action."

"Given the evidence we've already provided," Scott said, "how is that not an overreaction, sir?"

"Because it's been over twelve hours since a cruise missile was launched at a major US city, and so far, our nation's only response has been to shake our fist and say, 'You'd better not do that again.'"

Jason shook his head. "But, sir, think about what you're say—"

"I have. And I need to do what's best for the American people. That's my job—to secure our best interests. And right now, it's evident that our national security is at risk. Twenty-four hours. After that, no more sitting on our hands."

TWENTY-ONE

AN HOUR PASSED since they'd ended the call with the president and Joint Chiefs, and all they'd managed to do was reiterate what the problem was. It all hinged on Cipher. The mysterious criminal mastermind was the key to figuring the whole thing out. If they could track him down and get him to talk, maybe they could figure out who the real culprit was behind the intricate scheme. But they'd have to do all of that before the clock ran out, and now they only had twenty-three hours to pull off the seemingly impossible.

The CIA had yet to get back to them. Nor had the FBI, NSA, or the United Nations Security Council. Everywhere they checked, everyone they spoke to, they got the same thing: Cipher was a ghost. An apparition. A phantom of the dark web that many even denied the existence of.

"Of course, some of them deny it," Murph said when they got back in touch with the hacker. "It's self-preservation, right? Who the hell would want to admit that somebody like him exists? Not exactly a recipe for sleeping easy at night. But wishful thinking doesn't change the fact that he's real and that he's the one responsible for everything."

"What can you tell us about him, Murph?" Jason said.

"First off, let me start by saying that the systems at Tenth Circle were locked up tight. Real tight. Some of the best security I've seen anywhere. Which was why my first reaction when I heard the news was that it'd been an inside job—that somebody working at Tenth Circle had been bought off or something. But after hours of poring over the intel I was given from the facility, it became clear that the facility was indeed hacked, which is nearly impossible. So, whoever hacked into it, he's as good or better than me. I can say with no ego that I'm one of the top five best hackers in the world, and I personally know three of the others."

"What about the last one?"

"You're jumping ahead. Next, there was an attack on an Iranian weapons facility a few months ago . . . It was flawless. I'm telling you, I really get into these kinds of things. I delve deep into what happened and how. Again, the weapons facility's network was hacked. Completely hijacked. A state-of-the-art, top-tier weapons facility at the mercy of a guy and his computer, and two cruise missiles were stolen. What happened that day requires a level of expertise bordering on supernatural. And both that incident and the Tenth Circle hacking job reek of the same culprit."

"Let me guess . . . this Cipher guy?"

"That's right."

Scott said, "Any idea where we can find him?"

The hacker paused, then let out a chuckle. "What, you think I'm gonna have his full real name and address handy? This guy's a ghost. The real deal. He's as good a hacker as me, but he's far more dangerous than I am because Cipher doesn't hold himself to any kind of code. No moral standard. He'll do what he wants to do, when he wants to do it, with no regard for the consequences. And in addition to being a top-level hacker, he's a brilliant military strategist. Imagine a battle as a game of chess and this guy's Garry Kasparov. I can't think of another person alive who could pull off these two hacking jobs. And it sounds like, based on what that hitman said to you, Jase, that Cipher wanted you to know he's after you. It's part of one of his twisted mind games, I guess."

"There must be some way we can find him," Jason said.

"Have you been listening? This guy's a damn mirage. And he knows all about you. Trust me. By now, I'm sure he knows about all of you. Hell, he could even be listening in on this call."

"It's a secure line," Scott said.

Murph laughed again. "When it comes to Cipher, nothing is secure. Trust me."

Jason folded his arms. "You make him out to be nonhuman."

"Oh, he's human. Barely."

"You've got nothing to go on, Murph?" Jason said. "We're empty-handed here. There's no plan to find this guy aside from waiting for more highly trained killers to show up—and try to blow my head off—and hoping we capture one of them for questioning, only to find out they die before they talk because they're scared shitless of this Cipher guy."

"I don't blame them for being terrified. So am I."

Jason shook his head and stood taller. "Pull it together, Murph. If we can't count on you when things get bleak, then what the hell kind of man are you? Yeah, I get it. It's risky. But you know what's even riskier? Sitting on the sidelines. Cowering in fear because the big bad wolf behind his computer might make you his next target. He's human, Murph. Whoever the hell he is, he's human. And you know what I'm gonna do? I'm gonna track his human ass down. And after he tells me who hired him, I'm gonna put a bullet through his skull."

The line fell silent. Jason paced the room, feeling the clock winding down and ticking toward inevitable war.

"I may have a contact who can help," Murph said. "They're with the CIA and have been after Cipher for a long time. This agent reached out to me a couple years back, and I basically said the same thing I'm telling you guys now. But I've heard through the grapevine that they may have something. It could be hearsay, so don't count on it, but I'll try to get in touch. Other than that, I really have nothing to go on."

Jason calmed, planting his hands on the table and relaxing his breathing.

Scott rubbed the back of his neck. "Thanks, Murph. We hope to hear back from you soon."

Feeling as low as he'd ever felt in his life, Jason headed topside for some fresh air. The worst part was feeling useless—like whatever was about to happen was out of his control. But he remembered a powerful lesson he'd been taught by a man he'd revered:

"A man is defined by how he handles his darkest moments."

And so he took in a deep breath, then headed back inside. He'd only been gone five minutes, but the mood in the control room had visibly shifted when he returned.

"Murph got ahold of his contact," Scott said. "And they already happened to be in South Florida. They're on their way here."

An hour later, a Sikorsky Black Hawk UH-60 helicopter eased down onto the *Valiant*'s helipad. The team didn't know what to expect, but they were all caught off guard when a blond woman, who was barely over five feet tall and a hundred pounds, stepped down from the aircraft.

CIA Special Agent Kate Royal was wearing a black suit and sunglasses as she moved swiftly toward the base of the superstructure. Part of the Agency's Special Activities Division, Royal had still been at the hospital being stitched up when she received the urgent call from Murph.

"This way, Agent Royal," Scott said, ushering her into the control room.

Despite her stature, Royal had a commanding, authoritative presence about her. She was all-focus when she stepped into the space and rested her shoulder bag on a chair.

"I don't want this to come across the wrong way," Scott said, "but the Agency's had you hunting this guy for five years, and he's still at large?"

"It hasn't been an official manhunt," she stated matter-of-factly. "He's just been on our wanted list."

"So, *you've* been hunting him?" Jason said. "On your own time?"

She said nothing, which was as good as an answer in the affirmative.

"Why?" Jason added.

"Let's just say I've got personal reasons for wanting to take Cipher down. Personal reasons that have now been amplified by the fact that my partner for the past four years was just killed right in front of me in an attack Cipher no doubt orchestrated."

"Again, don't take this the wrong way," Scott said, "but you flew all the way out here just to tell us this? Wouldn't a phone call have sufficed?"

"I came out here because I want to help. I have a lead on how we might be able to find him. It's far from a sure thing, and it's daring, but that's why I wanted your team's help. As of this moment, there are only two people who've ever survived an attack planned by Cipher. You and me," she said, eyeing Jason. "And yours was an assassination attempt with multiple stages. You shouldn't be alive, and you are. That's saying something. I've heard a little of your group's past exploits, and you have good ties with Murph. Better than the Agency does. If we work together, I think we might be able to find this guy."

The room filled with nods and subtle gestures.

Scott, reading the consensus of his team, said, "What's this possible lead?"

He had contingencies in place, of course. Backup plans to take into account the ever-present variable of human error. But even some of the contingencies had failed, and some key targets had slipped through the cracks and were threatening the whole thing.

It doesn't matter, he told himself.

He had it all under control. He was always multiple steps ahead of them. That was the key. Being so far ahead and knowing their actions before they do, you can lead them on. You can drop little crumbs and lure them in the direction of your choosing. Dish out illusions of false hope and progress. Make your adversaries think they're on to something, only for them to find out later on that they were very wrong.

The hooded man grinned and shifted from screen to screen. His mind at work, multiple steps ahead, he relished the slight challenge and what he knew would ultimately lead to an even more rewarding outcome.

TWENTY-TWO

VERKHOYANSK MOUNTAIN RANGE, SIBERIA

OFFICIALLY, THEIR DESTINATION didn't exist.

It's what is known as a black site—a term used to describe a place where an unacknowledged black operation is being conducted.

After taking off from the *Valiant* in The Bahamas, Jason and Agent Royal had spent four hours aboard the group's supersonic jet and covered over six thousand miles. The CIA operative hadn't been exaggerating about her lead being far from a sure thing.

Back in the control room, she'd explained how six months earlier, the Kremlin had been the victim of its own cyber warfare attack. The man responsible, a Russian professor named Vladimir Petrov, was captured within twenty-four hours of the crime in a joint operation with foreign stationed CIA operatives. Royal was one of the agents who flew abroad to aid in the search, but the professor was taken into custody and swept off to a secret holding facility before any foreign service members could interrogate him.

"I have good reason to believe that this professor didn't perform the attack on his own," Royal explained. "I believe, and Murph can back me up on this, that he was working with Cipher. And that maybe, just maybe, he might know where we can find the reclusive criminal. But I never had the chance to question him."

She went deeper into her theory, then explained how she'd been fighting to be granted a meeting with the professor, but all her attempts had fallen on deaf ears.

Once the team was convinced that Royal's lead was their only option, Scott made a call to the president. At its best, U.S.–Russia relations are a potent mixture of cooperation and competition, and the act of balancing the two has often led to skewing of information and outright deception. But the current situation had changed things. Important calls were made, and Jason and Royal were granted permission to meet with the man the Russian government dubbed "the deranged professor."

They first flew to the town of Batagay, where they transferred onto a Russian helicopter for the trip into the mountains of the Sakha Republic. Their destination, which was located in a region the size of India but with a population of less than a million people, was surrounded by hundreds of miles of some of the emptiest, coldest, and harshest tundra found anywhere on Earth.

Jason gazed out the window as the helicopter soared over endless peaks covered in thick snow, until they eventually descended along the leeward side of a mountain. Flurries of white blew back as the chopper eased down onto a concrete pad painted white to blend in nearly perfectly with the environment.

"Gloves on," a Russian federal agent said, the first word he'd spoken since they boarded the helicopter nearly an hour earlier.

He was their primary escort, along with two high-ranking Russian soldiers. The man was tall and wide-shouldered. He had a permanent scowl on his face and wore a long, thick arctic coat and a fur ushanka hat, along with heavy pants and big boots. Jason and Royal had been given similar attire back in Batagay, and they did as the man said and slid on their thick gloves as the rotors slowed.

The side door opened without warning, and a powerful snowdrift howled into the cabin. The frigid air bit at uncovered skin, and as they climbed out, blinding rays of sunlight reflected back at them from the never-ending white. During the journey, Jason and Royal had skipped forward across thirteen time zones. It was now high noon in the Siberian province, and the late-December sun was blinding.

They followed the Russian agent down through the door and across the pad, shielding their faces from the relentless wind. Pushing into the shadow of the steep mountainside before them, they got their first look at the classified location. From the outside, the only portions visible were a big metal door and concrete walls painted in camouflaged streaks of black and white.

Built right into the mountain and boring deep at the site of a former mine, the place had a history as dark as its present. The mine, like many in the region, had been worked by prisoners. It was part of the famous gulags—political prisoners and criminals of the Soviet Union, enemies of the regime charged without trial and sentenced to a fate far worse than imprisonment.

Jason remembered learning that at its height, the Soviet Union had rounded up millions of people for use in their harsh labor camps, most of whom died from the extreme conditions. Just looking at the outer rock walls of the facility gave him a slight chill as they pushed through snow toward the door leading into the concrete structure.

The Russian agent led them to the base of the entrance. With concrete walls five feet thick, it looked more like a bomb shelter or a secret nuclear missile silo.

The lead Russian stopped at the right side of the door. He slid his hand free from his glove and pressed a barely visible button that was flush with the concrete. A tiny cover slid up, revealing a touchpad. He blocked himself with his thick coat as he punched in a long series of numbers. A security camera situated above the touchpad zoomed in, and he stared at it a moment while sliding his cap up for facial recognition.

The cover slid back over the keypad, and the door slid open slowly. The Russian led the way, the two soldiers sticking to Jason and Royal's flanks.

They were taken to the center of a small room, where half a dozen men stood by, forming a half circle. Two of them stepped forward and frisked everyone who'd arrived, including the two soldiers and the agent. They scanned metal detectors over every inch of them and patted them down.

After the thorough search, they were escorted into an adjoining room with an elevator.

The agent led them inside, then pressed one of the lower buttons. "He's on the lowest prisoner level," the big Russian said.

Jason counted five levels between where they entered and where they were heading and wondered what the others were for. Jason and Royal's presence was making the Russians uncomfortable, that was for sure. It was something far out of the ordinary. The classified Siberian prison wasn't exactly a place that offered tours. He imagined no foreigner had entered the facility since it'd been constructed—not since miners had worked the cold, dark shafts.

The elevator was faster and smoother than Jason expected, and the mechanism soon slowed to a stop. The doors parted, revealing a space with folding chairs and steel counters. More men stood and watched as they passed by. The entourage grew again as they were led through two locked doors, the agent leading the way and swiping his key cards.

The cell block was short, but the cells were well-spaced.

"At first, he was kept one level up," the agent explained. "With the most dangerous threats. Lifers. But problems arose."

"What kinds of problems?" Royal asked.

"Safety and security problems."

Jason raised his eyebrows. "He was attacked by other inmates?"

"No. The prisoners here are kept in permanent solitary. Doctor Petrov was never attacked, but he was able to communicate through the bars. We grew concerned for the inmates and the guards."

"How could he hurt anyone if he was locked up all day?" Royal said.

The man hesitated a moment, as if it was hard to explain—as if it was something you had to see for yourself to believe.

"He's a manipulator," the agent said. "A convincing one. He had the other inmates listening to him and believing him. Then he got some of the guards on his side."

Royal raised her eyebrows. "The guards did what he said?"

"Like I told you, he's an efficient manipulator. So, we got rid of those guards, and we put him here in complete solitary."

"How long's he been down here?" Jason asked.

"Two months. He hasn't even seen another person in that time and gets his food through a tiny door."

"I'm assuming he was interrogated after he was captured?" Royal said.

"You assume correctly."

"Did you learn anything?"

"We don't comment on classified affairs, but no, he didn't say a word that wasn't intended to secure his freedom—as I'm sure will be the case when he talks with you two."

They pushed through yet another thick door that opened following a beep. At the end of the hall was a solid gray door with a thin tray hole at the bottom.

"I don't know who you talked to or what they said to get you two clearance to come down here, but I don't like it. You've got thirty minutes with him. Not a second more."

He flashed his key card again. Since arriving, the whole trek had been a blur of one checkpoint after another. Bolts clicked away from the cell door, and the man heaved it open.

The cramped room had a cot, a toilet, and a couple of stacked books on the floor. But the cell was spotless, and there were lines of tiny text, numbers, and symbols all over the walls—advanced mathematical equations and theorems.

Dr. Petrov sat in the middle of the floor, his legs folded, his back straight, and his eyes closed. His three-inch beard was more black than gray, and scraggly hair was tied back in a loose ponytail. His face was clean and his clothes well kept. The cell didn't have an odor beyond the normal stale air from being that deep into the Earth's crust, relying on subpar ventilation. On the floor in front of him was a worn copy of *Meditations* by Marcus Aurelius.

"Dr. Petrov, these two are going to ask you some questions."

The man replied only by slowly opening his piercing green eyes and giving the higher-up a slight nod. Then he closed them again.

The Russian sighed. "You've got thirty minutes," he whispered, then stepped out of the cell.

"Can you shut it?" Jason said. The man shook his head, so Jason added, "We were told we'd be given a private conversation with him. Or would you like us to call our president and get this thing cleared up?"

The man stared back at Jason a moment, grunted, then shut the door. He clicked it in place but left it unlocked.

"It's peaceful in here, really," Dr. Petrov said calmly. "If you think hard enough . . . If you really concentrate . . . You can take your mind outside of these walls. Have either of you ever heard of mental transmutation?"

"We're here on important business, and we don't have time for chitchat," Jason said.

The professor remained perfectly still, then said, "American. Highly educated. Not with law enforcement. And a special agent with the CIA. This ought to be interesting." He opened his eyes and cast his piercing gaze straight at Agent Royal. "I never forget a face. You were there the night I was captured, and now you're here. You must have powerful friends." His eyes drifted over to Jason. "Or maybe he does."

His voice was smooth and articulate and oozed intelligence. It was like they were meeting the professor in his office at a distinguished university, not a hundred feet underground in a classified prison hundreds of miles from anywhere in the frozen Siberian mountains.

"We're looking for an accomplice of yours," Royal said. "We're looking for Cipher."

The man remained perfectly stoic. He closed his eyes again and breathed calmly. "A lie believed, even vehemently, doesn't make it anything else." He paused a beat, then continued. "We were never accomplices. He was a former student of mine, long ago, back when I first began teaching. He was bright and ambitious, but . . . unstable."

"What's his real name?" Jason asked.

"Symon Marchenko," Petrov said. "And he was brilliant. The best student I ever had. A prodigy who was doing advanced mathematics before he was ten years old. He did it for fun, he once told me."

Jason stowed the name in the back of his mind.

"No point remembering that name now. It won't help you."

"Why not?" Royal said.

"Because Symon Marchenko died in a car accident sixteen years ago. His car slid on the ice and crashed over a barrier into the Moskva River one dark February evening. Tragic. Or so the news reported it."

"You claim you weren't an accomplice," Royal said.

"No, I *stated* it. As a fact."

"You state you weren't an accomplice, but there's extensive evidence of your involvement in the hacking of the Kremlin's security system six months ago. Loads of data were extracted, and much of it was found on your personal computer. How do you explain that?"

"Like I said, he was the best student I ever had. The best at calculating and problem solving. Coding and designing. Formulating and executing intricate solutions."

"He framed you?" Royal said.

The man said nothing.

"When did you last hear from him?" Jason said. "Was there any contact after his disappearance?"

"Seven months ago. Just a couple weeks before the security breach. I sat down at my desk in Moscow, and there was a torn-up piece of paper resting there. It was an ink sketch of the constellation Andromeda, but it wasn't a normal drawing. The dimensions were exact, and the positions were perfect. I held it up to the light and examined it for ten minutes and even used a ruler. It was perfect. And I knew there was only one person who could've left it. You see, Symon had an unusual fascination with constellations. He used to doodle them all the time. Pegasus, Lyre, Charioteer . . . . It was a little obsession of his. He told me once he'd often close his eyes and visualize the night stars—that he worked to see patterns and mathematical symmetry in their placements, the same way he did for lines of code or equations or proofs."

The professor paused a long moment, then continued, "So, I checked an astronomical calendar and saw that Andromeda would be visible that evening. I went to our favorite spot in Sparrow Hills, a short walk from campus. He used to stargaze on a lesser-known crest surrounded by forest and rock outcroppings, and I'd joined him a couple times. I hoped to run into him, but instead, I found a note in the narrow crook of a rock face. I replied to it, and our communications went on like that for two weeks. Then I show up to work one morning, and I'm swarmed by police and foreign agents. You were there, Agent Royal."

"I never told you my name."

"No, you didn't."

Royal paced back and forth, thinking hard. "There are pictures of you in one of the drain tunnels beside the Kremlin," she said. "They showed you attaching a hacking device to one of the satellite security lines. How do you explain that?"

"Like I've told you . . . He was good. And more unstable than any of us knew."

Figuring out whether or not the guy was guilty wasn't going to get them anywhere. They needed info on Cipher's whereabouts, and they needed it fast.

"We need to find him, professor," Jason said. "He's on to bigger schemes. Ones with dire consequences for the world. We're talking millions of people affected. Do you have any idea where he might be?"

Petrov closed his eyes again. "I couldn't believe it. Part of me still can't. I guess that's part of being a teacher. You always hope for the best with your students. Or at least, you should. He was always so bright."

Jason checked his watch. They had five minutes left until they'd be ushered out of there, the tiny window of opportunity slamming shut moments after opening.

"Where is he, Petrov?" Jason said.

"Always bright. Loved his constellations. Especially the Southern Cross. And meteor showers. He was always looking for the best places to watch them."

"Where is he?" Jason said again, his temper rising.

Every time the second hand clicked, it felt louder and louder, and Jason's heart thumped stronger.

"And his minor was German Gothic architecture. He was fascinated with it. Especially the castles. He always—"

"Where is he?" Jason shouted, grabbing a fistful of Petrov's shirt and jerking him off the floor.

Jason could see Marcus in his mind. He could feel the raging water back in Texas and see his dead mentor's bullet-riddled body. He could feel the pressure of the impending crisis closing down on him.

Petrov's eyes sprang open, and he stared intensely at Jason and whispered, "I already told you."

"What?"

"I . . . I can't tell you. He'll kill me."

"How can he get to you in here?"

"Like I said, he's—"

"The best you ever taught. Yeah, I know. All I ever hear is how this guy's some kind of mythical monster mastermind who's uncatchable. But none of that matters because I'm going to catch him. Don't you realize we can help get you out of here? Do you want to spend the rest of your life in this miserable cell?"

Petrov gasped, then the door sucked open. Jason loosened his grip, lowering him to the floor.

"Time's up," the Russian said, marching inside. "I thought we told you not to touch him?" He grabbed Jason by an arm and pried him off the professor.

The prisoner spoke a final time as Jason and Royal were ushered out, his words clear and his tone calm. "I already told you where he is."

TWENTY-THREE

JASON STARED AT the metal door, the professor's words still lingering. "We need more time with him," Jason said, yanking his arm free of the Russian and stepping toward the closed cell.

The agent jammed the bolt shut, then clicked the other lock into place.

"We need to get back in there," Jason added, raising his voice.

The hard man turned to face Jason, his features hard and unaffected. "Your time is up," he said, motioning them to move down the hall.

Jason didn't budge. "We need more of it."

"Too bad. This way."

"Do you have any idea what's happening? What's at stake right now? We need to—"

The imposing man hovered his hand over his waist, his pistol, baton, and handcuffs conveniently lined up and ready to be utilized at a moment's notice. "You were granted thirty minutes. That time has elapsed." He grabbed Jason by the arm and squeezed tight again. Jason would've broken his arm and snatched the keys if they weren't surrounded by armed personnel.

"It's time to go," the agent said again, pulling him along.

Jason jerked his arm free once more, and the two soldiers closed in on his flanks, practically pushing him and Royal down the hall. They exited, and the Russian locked the door behind them.

"I'll be given more time," Jason said. "One call, and you'll have to grant me more time with him."

The Russian held his hands up. "You're welcome to call whoever you want, but you're not doing it here. You're both leaving now." The big man chuckled. "Not that it matters. I told you, he's a manipulator. A compulsive liar. He says whatever he needs to say to get you on his side."

They made it back five levels up and weaved out to the main door. Jason and Royal shot each other looks as they adjusted their coats and put on their gloves and hats.

Before sliding the thick fabric of the glove over his left forearm, Jason focused on the timer counting down. Fourteen hours remained, and Jason felt like they were no closer to figuring out who was really behind the attacks.

The towering outer door groaned and slid aside. A blinding white world came into view, swirls of snow howling inside. They stepped out, their boots thumping along the concrete to where their ride was still resting on the helipad. The sun was now about sixty degrees above the southwestern horizon, yet another reminder that time was passing by. The world—and everything in it—was continuing to move along, ticking their time away.

Inside the helicopter, the Russian higher-up said nothing as he faced forward in the seat in front of them. Jason had the left rear seat, facing out through the back left side window, and the two soldiers sat alongside he and Royal.

The pilots fired up the engines, gave them a little time to warm up, then pushed the rotors and took off shakily into the air. They cruised up to a thousand feet and soared east. Jason looked back as the visible portion of the facility grew smaller, then it quickly vanished in the sheets of rolling snowdrifts—the place blending into the mountainside and disappearing into the sea of nearly identical, white-coated peaks.

He thought about discussing what had happened with Royal but didn't want the others listening in. And they would be. So he just listened to the thumping of the rotors and engines and the screaming wind rushing by.

He thought hard about their conversation with the professor. It'd only been thirty minutes, but it felt far quicker than that. Like they were just warming up when the door opened at their backs.

What the hell are you supposed to get out of someone in thirty minutes?

He closed his eyes and thought about everything the prisoner had said, running through every single word in his memory, then picturing the professor and his cell. For the most part, it was a pretty simple conversation, but some things didn't make sense. Some variables didn't belong in the equation. Everything about the man had been neat and organized and precise. The way his bed had been made—the length of the blanket's edges perfectly tucked and folded over at the top and the pillow flat and carefully aligned. Everything was crisp and intricate, including the near-perfect script on the walls. Even his prison clothes and hygiene had been as best as Jason imagined they could be, given the circumstances. There was nothing random or chaotic about the guy.

So, why the sudden incoherency? Why the drastic shift to pointless chatter and useless facts?

"I already told you where he is."

The words wouldn't stop running through Jason's mind. The man's voice wouldn't go away. It was calm, collected, educated.

Manipulative.

The Russian agent's words elbowed their way into his thoughts as well, pleading their case.

Maybe he was just manipulating me. Maybe everything he said was a lie. But to what end? For what purpose?

Jason wore himself out overthinking and reaching and second-guessing. He checked the time and sighed. In ten minutes, they were going to land. They'd disembark and board the jet and would need a destination. And the last thing Jason wanted was to return to where they'd come. Back to the *Valiant*, empty-handed and with nothing to show for the wasted hours except for more questions.

"I already told you where he is."

He focused on the name of the man's former student and the incident sixteen years before. The Moskva River . . . That's where Symon Marchenko had supposedly crashed.

Is that it? Is he trying to tell me that Cipher is back in Moscow? That the guy has some strange connection to the place where he faked his death? The place where his old self had died, and he'd made the transformation into the notorious, criminal hacker he'd become?

It was possible, and more than that, it was probable. The professor claimed he'd already told them where Cipher was, and only two locations were mentioned during their conversation: the Moskva River and the Sparrow Hills—the place where Cipher had left the note—the place he used a sketch of a constellation to trick Petrov into communications in order to set him up for some reason. Either way, both places were located in the Russian capital.

He was about to turn to Royal and tell her his theory when the helicopter began to descend. The sun was already arcing down, and in a couple hours, it would slip beyond the horizon, casting the barren world into blackness.

Jason shivered just thinking about it. The place was bitterly cold in the middle of the day. He couldn't fathom what it was like at night, especially with the skies as clear as they were. But he imagined it was breathtaking out there. No light pollution. No obstructions. No unnatural sounds or distractions.

He pictured an inky black sky flooded with stars as they descended toward the airport. Then a new theory clicked in his mind, and he gasped and turned to Agent Royal.

TWENTY-FOUR

SEOUL, SOUTH KOREA

ELLIOT "MURPH" MURPHY knew he was being followed.

The realization came like a sucker punch to the gut.

The sky above was dark, but the world around him was bright and lively, a tightly packed network of tall buildings, dazzling lights, and flocks of tourists and locals alike.

The notorious hacker took great pride in his ability to remain anonymous, never staying in one place for longer than a week or two. Sticking to the dense tourist areas where he could blend in with the hordes. Using fake identities while traveling, then different fake identities while checking in to hotels. Always paying cash, often changing up his look, and rarely going out during daylight hours.

It was a system that had served him well for the past four years, ever since he'd gone rogue from the NSA. He traded in his restrictive government career for private freelance work, where he picked the jobs. In those four years, he'd never been found. But that evening in the Myeong-dong district of Seoul, he knew without a shadow of a doubt that he was being followed.

He was on his way back to his hotel room after stopping at a little-known Korean street restaurant—one of his favorite places to eat on Earth. The eatery had a big counter along the sidewalk that allowed you to order and pay and get your food all in under thirty seconds.

He held the plastic bag of Korean sausage, spicy stir-fried rice cakes, and dumplings trapped in Styrofoam containers. It was less than a block after grabbing his food that he realized he had a tail, and his first reaction was to dip into the nearest crowd.

Murph possessed a high level of intelligence. He knew what his strengths were, but just as important, he knew his weaknesses. He aided men of action all the time, helping to locate enemies and infiltrate hostile locations from behind the scenes, while others pounded evildoers into submission. But that wasn't Murph. At a hundred and fifty pounds soaking wet, he was practically useless in a hand-to-hand fight. So, he stuck to his strengths and relied on anonymity, stealth, and deception. And in the unlikely event someone found him, he'd run.

He slipped to an adjacent sidewalk and zig-zagged his way across another street, threading between thousands of people heading in various directions.

He covered a hundred yards through the heart of the densely packed shopping district that saw over a million visitors pass through every day. Stealing a glance over his shoulder, Murph spotted his tail again. The man looked Korean and was dressed in a business-casual outfit with dark shades. He was medium height and clean cut, and he moved with a smooth, relaxed gait. Not former military, but confident and composed enough to clearly know what he was doing.

Not only was the stranger still following him, but the guy had somehow managed to close the distance a little. Murph crossed a busy intersection and hastened into a courtyard flanked by ginkgo trees. He dropped his food in a trash can, picked up his pace, and cut behind a tall hedge. He turned again, crouching as he raced along a decorative wall, then popped back into a street between two food stands.

He weaved through a busy block, then doubled back again at the next intersection, performing a circle of three left turns from where he'd originally spotted the tail. He shot a glance over his shoulder, then his heart rate picked up more.

The man was still there. He'd stuck with Murph beat for beat, and again, he managed to close the distance even more.

The guy was proficient—an experienced, well-trained stalker. And in Murph's experience, the art of proficient stalking was rarely a one-man job.

With his first two modes of escape having failed, he moved into his last resort. Plainly, it involved putting as much distance as he could between him and his stalker as quickly as possible. By the looks of the guy, Murph reasoned he wasn't going to be winning any footraces against him anytime soon, so he cut across the next intersection, then picked up his pace, trying his best to make it look natural. Another block up, he turned right, moving out of his stalker's line of sight.

The moment he was clear, Murph took off. He pumped his arms and sprinted as fast as he could. He flew around the next corner, waved his arms like mad, and whistled, flagging down a taxi. The sedan swerved off the road and braked to a stop. Murph nearly collided with the frame as he grabbed the rear door, his hands shaking. He jerked it open, then strong arms grabbed him from behind. They pulled hard, dragging his feet along the pavement.

Muscles hard as steel tightened against his windpipe and contorted his body back. Murph flailed, trying to break free with everything he had. He heard a chorus of gasps from nearby pedestrians and then a door sliding open. Everything went dark as he was heaved into a van, and a sack was thrown over his head.

TWENTY-FIVE

JASON DIDN'T HAVE time to bounce his idea off Royal. The bird was just about to touch down, and the wind had picked up even more, so they rocked and teetered. And if they communicated via the onboard headsets, the Russian higher-up would be listening in.

Instead, he just ran over the theory in his mind and tried to keep it fresh as they dropped to a shaky landing and the rotors wound down. The engine shut off, and the side door opened, letting a powerful surge of wind blast into the cabin. After climbing down, they headed straight for the parked jet. They'd called ahead, and it was warmed up and ready as they climbed aboard.

"We'll have a heading in five minutes," he told the pilots before rushing back to the small table and chairs.

"We will?" Royal said.

He nodded, then grabbed his laptop and cracked it open. "I think I might've figured out what Professor Petrov meant when he said he'd already told us where Cipher is."

She looked back at him skeptically, then Jason punched in the code and brought up a secured internet browser. "How many times do you think he said the word 'constellation'?"

She paused, taken aback by the seemingly random question. "I don't know."

"Ballpark figure. At least half a dozen times, right?"

"Maybe."

He typed ferociously.

"What are you searching?" she said, leaning beside him.

"He said the Southern Cross was his favorite. Cipher's, or Marchenko's favorite constellation was the Crux. Now, why did he tell us that? It's useless gibberish, right? Seems like it anyway. Seems like something a guy who's spent a little too much time in solitary confinement would say."

"Maybe he has."

"Or maybe he was trying to tell us something without telling us. Maybe he was trying to give us Cipher's position indirectly."

Jason kept his eyes locked on the screen, running over lines of text and pictures. "The Southern Cross is visible all year round in the southern hemisphere, at thirty-four degrees south and below."

Jason clicked open another tab and brought up a GPS image of Earth. He typed, then a dotted line appeared, running along the thirty-fourth parallel south and cutting through parts of South America, South Africa, and Australia.

"That doesn't exactly narrow it down enough."

"But wait," Jason said. "What else did the professor say? He mentioned that Marchenko never missed a meteor shower."

Jason opened a third tab and typed like mad, hoping his hunch didn't run him into a dead end. He scrolled down. "The peak of the Phoenicids meteor shower is expected to be visible tomorrow evening and it's best observed in the Southern Hemisphere, with clusters specifically centering around the southern tip of Africa."

Jason clicked back open the GPS tab and ran his fingers along the line. He stopped at South Africa. The thirty-fourth parallel line ran right through the heart of Cape Town, and the meteor shower was expected to be best viewed in that area at ten at night, local time."

Royal said, "This is progress, but how do we find him once we're there?"

Jason took half a minute to run through his searches, then moved forward and told the pilots to get them to Cape Town International as quickly as possible.

When Jason returned to his seat, Royal had claimed it and was typing on the laptop. "He also liked Gothic-style German architecture," she said. "Didn't Petrov say it was Marchenko's minor?"

Jason smiled, then closed in and leaned over beside her. "The other seemingly random thing the professor told us."

Royal searched for examples of German Gothic architecture anywhere near Cape Town and the whole Cape Peninsula. Neither of them were optimistic anything clear-cut would reveal itself. Jason didn't know a lot about the country at the bottom of the African continent, but he did know that it was first settled by the Dutch and then the British. He figured if there was any German architectural influence, it would be minimal.

The search results proved him wrong immediately. The first thing to pop up was an exact replica of Lichtenstein Castle, the famous Gothic-style chateau in Southern Germany. Built in the late nineteen-nineties and overlooking Hout Bay, the castle was just eight miles southwest of Cape Town.

Bringing up the castle on the GPS, they saw that it was on a hill and had a wide-open view of the southern sky, right where the Crux constellation was best visible, along with the upcoming meteor shower.

They stared in silence at images of the castle, then Royal clicked open its website. She learned that the mansion was currently owned by an unknown Russian family that rented it out for private events.

Jason sat in the seat beside Royal as the jet's engines fired up and it taxied onto the apron. Royal pinched her lips as she stared at the screen, then paused and peered out the nearest window. She looked like she wanted to say something. Jason could see she was trying to work something out in her mind, and he let her work through it undisturbed.

They taxied out, accelerated right away on the lonely airstrip, and were shoved back into their seats as the powerful engines blasted them into the Siberian sky.

As they ascended, Royal turned to him. "Ok, let's say you're right about all of this. If Petrov was telling us where Cipher is, then that wasn't the only thing he was telling us. He was also indirectly telling us something else."

"Cipher's been communicating with him," Jason said.

Royal nodded. "Only thing I can figure . . . How else would Petrov have known where he was? Prior to our visit with him, I was expecting him to hopefully point us in the direction of one of Cipher's former hideouts or something, but he was too up to date for a guy kept in solitary confinement in the middle of a remote mountain. Someone somehow must've gotten the info delivered to him. I'm not sure how that's possible, but how else would he know that? There's got to be dozens of meteor showers a year, right? And around a hundred visible constellations? How could he possibly know where Cipher would be? And that German architecture bit? I'm willing to bet that wasn't Marchenko's minor."

"So, Cipher will know we're coming."

Royal leaned back, closed her eyes a moment, and sighed. "This whole thing. It's not adding up. If Petrov's story is true, then why would Cipher be communicating with him? And why would Petrov play along? You think he's scared of Cipher in there?"

"Maybe. And maybe he told us in code because that's what Cipher told him to do. Like he didn't want anyone else hearing it via the security camera."

"So, not only is Cipher supposedly renting out a German castle to watch a meteor shower during one of the boldest schemes of his life, but he also told us he's gonna be there? Why?"

Jason shook his head. "I don't know."

"And we're just going to head to this castle, even though he knows we're coming? That doesn't worry you?"

"No. All I care about is that we likely know where he is. And that's the first step in taking him down."

The time was drawing near. He could feel it. The realization gave him a sick form of satisfaction as he pictured a long fuse and a bright flame hissing as it burned toward a resting explosive. And the best part was, there was nothing anyone could do to stop it. It was far too late for that.

His smile broadened as he thought over his brilliant scheme. Controlling your enemies' actions was the key. Manipulation. Just like in chess. Force them to be reactive, then let them back themselves into a corner. Lead them away with a distraction, then execute the finishing touches on the master plan, uninhibited.

This would be his masterpiece—he was sure of that. His finest work.

His enemies had proven themselves more formidable than he'd anticipated, but that didn't matter. It only made the game more entertaining.

He stared at a man sitting in a leather chair with a sack over his head, and then he chuckled.

Yes, the scheme is just getting more enjoyable by the second.

A muscular man with a shaved head leaned over behind him. "The place is secured and ready."

"Double the number of armed guards," Cipher said. "I have a feeling we're going to have a few uninvited visitors stopping by to enjoy the show."

The man nodded and marched away.

Cipher leaned back and relaxed. They were in for a show, all right. Both in the heavens above and on the ground below. A show unlike any before.

He closed his eyes and pictured the burning fuse again, hearing the hissing sound as it neared the mound of explosives.

TWENTY-SIX

HOUT BAY, WESTERN CAPE, SOUTH AFRICA

THERE WAS ONLY one road leading to the castle. It snaked up for nearly a mile, weaving around short forests and opening to lush fields and dragon statues. Where the road began, there was a gate and two armed guards. Scott, Alejandra, and Royal were parked just down from the gate, ready to make a quick move on Jason's signal. Finn was piloting a surveillance drone, the little device having already completed a couple high-altitude laps around the compound, offering clear, zoomed-in footage of the castle and grounds.

Jason first heard the music when he stepped out of the car and started his rushed hike across the dark landscape. It'd been distant—barely a thumping hum at first—then grew louder as he'd made his way across the terrain. He figured most of Hout Bay could hear the powerful techno music blaring across the mountainside.

He'd been dropped off on the western edge of the town, right where the lines of houses ended at the base of the mountain. Dressed in black tactical gear, he trekked over a quarter mile up and along the steep slope, the darkness and thick foliage concealing his movements. He wore a bulletproof vest—a new design using thin, microscopically grooved Kevlar that was created by their team of engineers. He was armed with a Glock .45-caliber pistol, a Walther P22 with a suppressor, extra magazines for both, a fragmentation grenade, and various other gadgets. No one knew what to expect, so he came prepared to do some serious damage.

Wrapping along the upper portions of the mountainside, he reached a short ridge three hundred yards above the compound and crept out from the bushes, getting a clear look at the castle, its turrets dark against the verdant mountainside.

Set amongst a lush green backdrop, the highest structure on the Karbonkelberg hillside looked like a scene pulled right out of a fantasy novel—a medieval chateau surrounded by perfectly landscaped grounds and overlooking the sea.

Gazing upon the castle from his perched hiding place, he saw swarms of people surrounding the mansion, most of them concentrated around the pool area. Bright strobe lights flashed, and the music boomed even louder, the wild party before him anything but the quiet hideout they'd been expecting to find Cipher hunkering down in.

But as Jason looked closer, he saw that there was no shortage of security. At least a dozen men in suits stood stoically at the corners of the pool area and veranda, and there were at least another dozen near the driveway, main entrance, and scattered about the grounds. He'd seen lighter displays of armed personnel at high-value government facilities.

Jason checked the timer on his watch. Eight hours. That was all that remained until the conflict with Iran would severely escalate. Maybe they didn't even have that long. It'd been sixteen hours since they'd communicated with the president and the Joint Chiefs. A lot could've changed in that amount of time.

During the five-hour flight from Siberia across Asia, the Middle East, and the African continent to the Cape Peninsula, Jason and Royal had gotten ahold of the team aboard the *Valiant*. Scott orchestrated a rapid joint operation between US federal agents at the American consulate in Cape Town, South Africa's military, and the local police force.

Over thirty armed personnel and ten vehicles were ready, just beyond the gate to the castle's driveway. Private airstrips within a hundred-mile radius were shut down, so there was no way for Cipher to escape. Even with the extreme security presence, the guards at the castle would be no match for the assembled joint force.

But they needed Cipher alive. The whole thing was futile if they couldn't get him to talk. That was why Jason wanted to get to him first. Not just for everything the murderer had done, but to come through on a promise he made while Marcus's dead body was floating in his arms. He resolved to catch the renowned criminal and beat the truth out of him by whatever means necessary.

Jason breathed in the cool ocean air. It was some of the freshest he'd ever tasted, having blown from Antarctica over two thousand miles of ocean.

The world around him was pristine and mostly undeveloped. Solid black silhouettes of the nearby mountain peaks towered around him, and below was the silvery curve of a white sandy shoreline. Overhead, stars twinkled in thick clusters and reflected off the calm waters of the immense harbor.

Suddenly, bright streaks of light flashed across the sky and vanished a moment later. Then more appeared. The chatter at the castle grew louder, and people shouted and cheered and whistled and clapped.

The music remained loud, the heavy bass echoing across the mountainside and down through the valley, but the biggest strobe lights switched off, offering the guests clearer views of the spectacle.

Jason took the celestial event as his cue. He crawled back into the brush, then hustled down the mountainside toward the compound, keeping low and sticking to the shadows.

"We've got movement at the top of the tower," Finn said into his earpiece. "Zooming in for a better look."

Jason kept moving, then crawled as he neared the wall. Like the castle itself, the barrier was made out of large red bricks and was easily ten feet tall. The parapet was complete with regularly spaced out, squared openings, just like the ones medieval archers shot through.

Jason's phone buzzed softly. He slipped it out and eyed a picture Finn had sent. The image was taken from far away but with a powerful camera with good night vision and incredible zoom capability. It showed a pale-faced man in a black hoodie standing at the top of the tower and staring skyward with an intense gaze.

"Could be our guy," Finn said through the radio.

"We're running his face through facial recognition software now," Scott said. "If he's in any system around the world, we'll find him. Jason, what's your status?"

"At the wall now," he said, scanning the barrier.

"If we were looking for a good distraction to make our move, this is it," Scott said, referring to the meteor shower.

Jason knew it. He listened and heard the buzzing of an electric fence running along the top of the wall. There were eight lines of thin wire, spaced out inches apart and extending four feet over the top of the wall.

Remembering the map of the property, he headed northwest along the perimeter for fifty yards, then the barrier arched inward, and he spotted a back gate. It led to a footpath that wound up the hillside to a waterfall. Two guards were gazing out into the dark foliage with rifles strung across their chests.

Jason approached them, staggering his way along, making a lot of noise, and pretending he was intoxicated.

The two armed men snapped around and raised their weapons in fluid, synchronous motions. "Hands in the air!" one of them barked.

Jason froze and did as he was ordered, throwing his hands high above. He wobbled, then continued forward until he reached the edge of the path.

"Not another step," the guard shouted as they closed in.

"On your knees, now!" the other ordered.

The meteors continued streaking across the sky, and the music thumped and boomed, covering their barking words.

Jason stopped and dropped to the grass while keeping his hands up high. He swayed and coughed and looked up as the two guards closed in.

"Easy fellas," he said. "I was just taking a leak."

"How the hell did you get outside the walls?"

Jason grabbed the lead guard's weapon, jerked the barrel down over his shoulder, and socked him in the solar plexus. Using the guy as cover, Jason spun and bashed his leg into the side of the second guard's knee. He buckled and tumbled to the ground, and Jason knocked out the first guy with an elbow to his temple. Then he withdrew his knife and buried it into the second guard's neck just as his back hit the grass.

With both guards down, he rushed for the small back gate. Cracking the thick wooden door open, he peeked into the compound.

"I'm inside," he said into his radio.

"Nice moves," Finn said. "You've got two rovers inbound from the northwest, skirting along the inner side of the wall. And there are still at least six huddled near the parking lot and main entrance."

Jason hinged the door open another foot, then focused inside and spotted the two guards Finn was referring to. They were still a decent ways off but closing in fast. Turning left, he scanned the side of the towering structure and the trees and hedges surrounding it. A line of shadows stretched from his position to the backyard near the pool area.

Pushing the door open quietly, he took off, moving stealthily until he reached the backside of the property. Holding steady, he paused a moment and looked around. The music was deafening as he looked over the throngs of wild partygoers and intermixed guards. He shifted and eyed the frontal approach, where handfuls of armed men lulled about.

He made his choice, then said, "At the back of the castle and making my move."

Scott said, "Copy that, Jase. We're closing in from the west."

Jason pulled out his Walther P22 and screwed a suppressor onto the end of the barrel. Focusing on the back of the pool area, he was about to pounce from his hiding place when Finn's voice returned in his ear.

"There's movement in the turret," he said.

Jason angled his body and peered toward the top of the tower. A figure appeared, and he realized they were holding something. Reholstering his pistol, Jason slipped out his binos, focused the lenses, and saw the figure holding a sign.

His pulse quickened as he read the handwritten words.

If anyone but Wake steps foot on these grounds, Murph's dead.

TWENTY-SEVEN

JASON COULD FEEL the tension thickening in the air as he read the words. He watched through the lenses, his grip tightening on the frame as the sign lowered and a hooded man appeared.

Jason's phone buzzed. It was a phone call on his personal line—on the number he'd changed less than twenty-four hours earlier.

He slid out the phone and saw an unknown number. Peering back through the binos toward the top of the tower, a flash of a strobe light illuminated the mysterious man's pale face, along with a phone held up to his ear.

Jason answered and listened.

"Come out, come out, Jason Wake," the man said in a Russian accent. "It's time to play." He reached his hands for the sky and spread them out wide while gazing toward the escalating meteor shower. He briefly swayed to the music, then lowered the phone back to his ear. "I'm right here. Come and get me."

Jason's gaze tightened. "I'll be right there, Symon."

He tossed the burner phone into the brush. Reaching for his earpiece, he said, "Time to crash this party."

Keeping his pistol holstered, he rose from behind the hedge and strode across the yard, heading toward the chaotic pool area. Once across the grass, he slipped into the shadows, then walked casually under the balcony. He went for the guard standing beside the outer pillar first, jamming a hand into the guy's wrist as he tried to withdraw his sidearm. Jason covered his mouth and pounded his knuckles into the man's throat.

He let go, and the guard gagged as Jason hooked a hand behind his neck and jerked him down while driving up his right knee. The bone struck his forehead, and the guy went lifeless. As he crumpled to the ground, Jason moved on, wrapping around the pillar and cutting through an outer cluster of half-naked, intoxicated partiers, and cutting the distance to the next guard.

Jason swooped around and pounced from the blackness. He grabbed the guy by his shirt collar, swung hard, and pounded him headfirst into the wall. He collapsed just as a third guard appeared out of nowhere, growling as he stomped toward Jason. The hulking man threw two heaving punches, the air whooshing beside Jason's face as they flew by. He backed Jason into a corner, then the American managed to strike a heel into the guy's instep and pound a fist across his jaw.

Swiftly recovering, the guard grabbed his holstered pistol. Jason gripped his arm and shoved it skyward, and the guy fired two rounds into the sky before Jason spun him and threw him face-first into a fountain.

Twisting his arm around, Jason leveraged himself against a decorative stone dragon as the guard struggled and fought to break free. Soon, he went still in Jason's arms, dropped his pistol, and rested lifelessly, his body draped over the edge of the fountain.

In the chaos of the wild party, Jason spotted another guard closing in, his weapon already drawn and raised. Jason turned, using the drowned behemoth as cover as he snatched his suppressed Walther and took aim. He fired two rounds, one striking the guard in the chest and the other blasting into his forehead.

The music amped up as he shoved the big guy off him and broke into the heart of the party, his pistol raised as he headed for the opposite side. The security team mobilized near the base of the stairs scattered, sifting their way into the thick crowd.

People splashed wildly in the pool and danced all around him, flailing their arms and legs and whipping their hair. They brushed elbows and shoulders with him as he focused and pushed through. Glow sticks broke apart, the radiant fluid splashing everywhere. The smell of alcohol, sweat, and chlorine was heavy in the air, and steam rose from the heated pool, coating the scene in an ominous haze.

The pool area offered a perfect perched view of Hout Bay below and distant mountains at his back. His eyes darted from one person to the next, searching for his next threat.

A guard broke through the madness to his right. Jason dropped and spun and blasted a round into his foot, causing him to collapse forward. He fired another into his chest, then slid back and shoved the guy into the pool.

Two more steps, and another appeared, pouncing from his six with a blade arcing toward his right shoulder. Jason spotted him in his peripherals and dropped again, letting the knife stab right over his body. He snatched the guy's arm and used his opponent's own momentum to hurl him over his body and slam him into the deck. A kick to the side of the head put him to sleep, and Jason raised his pistol again, scanning and aiming as he threaded through the partygoers.

Though intoxicated, some of the people began to take notice—the occasional scream filling the air and bodies parting away from him as he reached the base of the stairs. A man at the top appeared with an assault rifle, and Jason dove behind a wall as he opened fire. The partiers screamed and scattered as the thundering rounds pelted the wall and banisters in front of Jason, blasting away pieces of brick.

Another guard appeared, this one stealthy and quick, like a striking cobra. He sprang out of the shadows, grabbed Jason from behind, and stabbed a syringe toward his throat. Jason caught the guy's wrist, and the two grappled, spinning and colliding into the wall. Pinning the syringe to the brick, Jason landed an elbow, then muscled the guy around, forcing the syringe free and stabbing it into the guard's gut.

The man's eyes bulged as Jason kept pushing, yelling as he ran the guy into a dark corner. Squatting, Jason heaved the man over his head and dropped him onto a bronze statue of a guard holding a spear. The tip pierced through the guy's chest, and he flailed, struggling to free himself.

His heart pounding, Jason took two big strides, then jumped off the wall. Reaching high overhead, he caught the corner of the veranda, pulled himself up high enough to hook his right foot, then rolled out under an embrasure.

His suppressed pistol was gone, so he retrieved his Glock and took down the guy with the rifle as he hustled down the stairs. He flipped forward with the blows and rolled violently to the base and the scattering people.

Jason caught his breath, his adrenaline pumping like mad. He felt possessed as he rapidly scanned the place with his handgun raised, then rushed toward a pair of big, propped-open side doors and into the castle. He passed an abandoned DJ booth, the music still screaming out the speakers and adding confusion to the scene.

People rushed out around him, racing for the parking lot as he moved inside. He entered a ballroom with high, painted ceilings and a sprawling black-and-white checkered floor. Mirrors running along the walls made the space appear even bigger than it was.

As people flooded out, the space dimmed, but the music continued to blare. When Jason was halfway across the room, an object flew toward him. He turned back, but before it even landed, the flashbang exploded, the sound blasting Jason's eardrums and blinding him in a powerful blaze of light.

Unable to see, Jason jumped back instinctively. He took cover behind one of the pillars and dropped low as his ears rang. He blinked rapidly, fighting to clear the blur from his eyes. The flash hadn't caught him straight on, but even the reflections of the intense light temporarily blinded him.

He poked around the corner and focused as best he could. A man was striding toward him from across the ballroom. His movements were familiar, but Jason couldn't trace the guy. That was, until he stepped into the light of the central chandelier.

Jason flashed back to Texas and the surprise attack at Tenth Circle. He and Marcus were surrounded near the edge of the cliff, and one of the assassins had stepped out from behind the boulders and took aim.

Still barely able to see, Jason looked around, then took off to his right toward a side door out of the ballroom. He just managed to swing it open and dart through when the man opened fire at his back, blasting a horde of pellets from his shotgun and splintering the door behind him to pieces.

TWENTY-EIGHT

SCOTT, ALEJANDRA, AND Agent Royal didn't give a damn about Cipher's threat. The stakes were too high, and Murph knew the risks of his involvement. They all did.

Dealing with the guards at the gate had been easy, and they were flying halfway up the winding road to the castle when cars began screaming toward them. They were mostly sports cars—exotic and shiny and packed with unnecessary horsepower. And they tore right passed the Suburban, fleeing for the exit.

"No one leaves the premises," Scott said into his radio.

"Yes, sir," a South African police officer replied immediately. "We have the exit blocked off."

Scott floored the gas, roaring them up the rest of the long driveway and slowing when the towering medieval structure came into view.

He didn't head for the parking lot. Instead, he veered off the road, plowing across the yard and skidding to a stop at the front of the mansion. Gunfire echoed across the landscape like rolling thunder, rising up over the raging music as the three jumped out.

With the main entryways flooded with armed guards and fleeing guests, they crept along the wall, under an intricate lattice of ivy, and into a courtyard with fountains, then they stopped beneath an archway. The three paused and looked around. They were on the opposite side of the castle, far from the gunfire and frantic partygoers.

Scott smiled as they focused on a portcullis above, the thick wooden grating set against the side of a footbridge and held in place by two big chains. But the bottom of it was even higher than he'd expected, and there was nothing nearby he could use to climb onto to reach it.

He dropped down and clasped his hands together, then eyed Alejandra. "Ready?"

She gave a quick nod, then stepped onto his hands and sprang skyward while Scott heaved her into the air. She caught firmly onto the crossbeams. Gripping tight, she pulled herself up with impressive upper body strength before snagging the footholds with her toes and climbing up the rest of the way.

She stopped just before the rim and looked around. "All clear," she said before muscling herself up and landing softly on the upper story walkway.

Royal went next, lunging onto Scott's hands and flying onto the portcullis. Strong and dexterous, the CIA operative scaled the grating with ease.

Just as she reached the top, two guards came rushing around the corner, both breathing heavily. They stared at Scott for half a second, then reached for their weapons. Scott sprang toward the first man to react, grabbing his gun hand by the wrist and driving a palm into his face. The guy opened fire, and Scott jerked him around as a trail of three shots blasted from the chamber. The middle bullet hit the guy's companion in the leg, causing him to yell and buckle to the ground.

Scott turned and pulled his hands down, breaking the guy's arm over his shoulder with a loud crack. Then he spun and hurled him head over heels, his body flipping before colliding into a lower stone walkway and tumbling lifelessly into the yard.

The second guard tried his best to recover, rising and taking aim with his weapon. Before he could fire, Scott knocked the pistol free, landed a solid punch to the guy's gut, then threw a powerful front kick that struck his jaw and sent him flying backward into a row of flowers. By the time Scott looked up, both Alejandra and Royal had vanished over the top of the upper wall.

TWENTY-NINE

JASON RACED DOWN a hall and pushed through another door, entering an expansive living space with a half-moon couch and a grand fireplace housing a crackling fire. A second shotgun blast echoed down the hall, and a wave of pellets crashed into the door behind Jason, sending splinters all over the room as he took cover behind the couch.

Still gripping his Glock, Jason rose from the back of the sofa and took aim just as the assassin appeared. But he was there and gone in a blink, diving and rolling into the room and taking cover at the opposite side as Jason opened fire. He let off two shots, and both missed, the rounds soaring over the killer's head. Jason heard the rapid sound of shells being loaded into place. They were smooth, quick movements—the kinds performed by an expert who'd done it thousands of times.

Jason opened fire again, this time blowing a hole through the fabric of the couch's armrest. The bullet tore through the leather and support beams. The assassin broke left, barely appearing in Jason's view before taking aim for retaliatory fire.

Jason had no choice but to take cover again, flattening his body against the stone floor as the assassin opened fire, bursting an army of tiny projectiles across the room. The corner of the couch blew apart, bits of fabric and wood and cushioning blasting away like confetti.

Jason army-crawled to the right, using the backside of the sofa for cover as his adversary nearly mirrored his movements on the other side. Taking aim in the narrow space under the couch, Jason opened fire, this time pelting four quick rounds along a steady line, hoping for a stray bullet to strike his enemy. But the skilled assassin dove again and rolled, putting them right across from each other with just six feet of couch between them.

Knowing that another blast from his attacker's shotgun would undoubtedly bring about his demise, Jason threw a Hail Mary and hurled himself over the top of the sofa. The assassin was just steadying himself following his brisk maneuver and arcing the barrel of his twelve-gauge toward Jason. Flying across the room in a blur, Jason reached ahead and swatted the weapon away with his left hand a fraction of a second before the assassin flexed his trigger finger. A fourth shell, deafening and powerful, exploded from the barrel, right past Jason as he collided into his opponent.

He tackled the assassin backward, the two crashing into the edge of the mantle. In a smooth act, the man shrugged off the blow, released his weapon, and knocked Jason's pistol free before he could bury a round in the guy's gut.

Jason threw a fist across the guy's face, but the assassin managed to create space by driving a knee into Jason's breadbasket, knocking the air from his lungs. The man swiped a micro handgun from his waistband as Jason drove forward, grabbing the guy by the wrist, his momentum sending them both into a spin along the edge of the crackling fireplace.

They stopped with the flames just a foot away from their hands, and Jason forced the gun toward the fire, muscling the guy's hand closer to the scorching heat. With the flames too intense to bear, the guy yelled as he let go of his pistol and then pounded his forehead into Jason's face. Jason tried to go with the blow, but it was fast and powerful, and it knocked him backward moments after the guy's pistol rattled into the heart of the fire.

Jason fell to the floor between the fireplace and the couch. The assassin recovered, then grabbed hold of a nearby fire poker and slammed it down. Jason rolled away from two powerful strikes of the iron slamming and sparking against the tile floor. Retreating beside a stack of firewood at the edge of the mantle, Jason turned and landed a kick to the outside of the guy's right knee. He buckled forward but caught himself on the couch and reared back for another swing of the iron rod. But before he could execute the attack, Jason seized a log from the stack and swung it with all the force he could muster. He slammed the timber into the assassin's head, a sharp nub from a split branch driving through the guy's skin and burying into his skull.

The man's eyes shot up, his body quivered, and he released control of the fire poker. Struggling to continue the fight, he reached for his knife as Jason jerked the log free, then landed a second blow, bashing the sharp, bloodied tip of wood into the corner of the assassin's right eye. He shook again and then fell back. Jason grabbed the fire poker and put him out of his misery with an adrenaline-fueled strike to the side of his head.

Jason let go of the heavy iron and staggered toward his pistol on the floor. He dropped to his knees, his body aching, his mind dazed, and his ears ringing as he grabbed the Glock.

He slid the mag out and replaced it with a fresh one. Placing a hand to his splitting head, he forced himself to his feet. Jason took a moment to run through the schematics of the castle and place himself in relation to the tower.

Keeping his eyes forward and his attention engrossed on the task at hand, he strode back toward the doorway, the assassin bloody and motionless at his back as he headed out toward a staircase.

THIRTY

ALEJANDRA FUENTES WAS no stranger to infiltrating mansions. As part of the anti-terrorism task unit in Venezuela for the past four years, she'd often been charged with sneaking into the compound of a high-value target with deep pockets.

A key she'd learned after years of infiltration was altitude—getting high up and swooping down on your enemies. Human peripherals have a biological bias programmed from years of fighting for survival on a planet full of creatures better equipped at deadly close encounters than we are. Most attacks on humans over the ages have come from eye level or below, so we've evolved to compensate.

The natural contour of the eye socket and skull make it slightly more difficult for humans to spot things that are above them, and it's also less expected, so when Alejandra came to a locked door, her instinct was to climb the nearby trellis.

She and Royal agreed to split up, and the CIA operative climbed over the right side of the wall and inched toward an open window on the second floor. They were both focused, blotting out the chaotic world below of rushing people, the throttling engines, the music, and the occasional gunshot coming from inside the castle.

Alejandra heaved herself onto the top, then held steady a moment while looking around. The roof was angled sharply on both sides but had a narrow, walkable stretch at its apex. She followed it halfway across, then scooted around the chimney, where smoke billowed out and faded away in the breeze.

Remembering the schematic, she headed for the master suite on the top floor of the castle. She reached another chimney that didn't have smoke pluming out, then she slid off her backpack, pulled out a harness, and swiftly tightened it around her body. Grabbing a coil of nylon climbing rope, she looped it snug around the brick chimney, then weaved it through the repelling mechanism of her harness. A skilled climber, she'd been summiting steep rockfaces since her father had taken her climbing as a kid.

She double-checked the loops and knots, then called in to Finn. "What's the status on the master?"

The Latino had the drone hovering just west of her position. "Heat signature reads three bodies still inside—one kneeling on the floor, the other two standing."

Alejandra inched toward the edge, then checked her holstered pistol and turned around. "Here we go," she whispered.

Keeping the rope taut, she leaned back and stepped over the edge, suspended sixty feet above the ground. She shifted her feet carefully, her body nearly perpendicular with the wall, until she reached the top of the largest of three stained glass windows in the master bedroom.

She waited there in the silence and shadows, taking intermittent glances at her watch. For nearly a minute, she remained as still as the statues littered across the grounds. A muffled explosion resonated from under the castle, and barely ten seconds later, all of the lights inside the mansion switched off.

Alejandra removed her pistol, gripping the weapon steady with her right hand and the rope with her left. Taking a deep breath, she bent her knees and then kicked off hard while loosening her grip on the rope. She soared backward and down, then tightened her grip on the rope as she dipped into the center of the window.

Her body jerked, and she swung forward. Arching herself back and lifting her boots up, she kicked again, this time her thick soles smashing into the center of the stained glass. The window shattered on impact, a deep crater that swiftly blossomed outward until the whole window turned to shards and burst into the room.

Alejandra released the rope, letting her body fly through the shards and across the space. She landed at the edge of a bed, the window crashing to the floor in a violent avalanche at her back.

The three figures were across from her—two men with their weapons drawn and standing beside a kneeling guy with a hood tied over his head.

She took aim before she'd landed and pulled the trigger the instant she could get off a steady shot. The closest guy went down before he knew what was happening. The second guy managed to drop back and fire an ill-aimed bullet toward the empty window frame behind Alejandra as she pulled the trigger twice more, the rounds pelting him center mass and knocking him into a corner.

Alejandra paused in the silent aftermath of her sudden entrance and attack. She remained in a crouched position, her body tucked behind the bed and her pistol aimed toward the door. She waited a couple seconds, listening and expecting backup to flood into the room at any second.

When none came, she rose, moving with light steps across the wooden floor as she traded her pistol for her knife and slashed the hood free. A quick jerk lifted it off, revealing a young man with a bloodied and bruise face. He looked like a college student with pimples, patches of short facial hair, and a plain gray T-shirt, the neck soaked with a mixture of sweat and blood.

He looked up toward Alejandra in a delirious daze.

"Murph?" she said.

The bound man blinked wildly, then gave a quick nod.

She'd never seen the notorious and reclusive hacker in person before. Even on video calls, his face was always covered or darkened. Up to that point, the man had been a shadow to her. An enigma. Someone who only existed on the internet, sitting behind a computer monitor in some hotel she'd never heard of in a city she'd likely never been to.

Now it was different. He was a person, ordinary and vulnerable and drained. Not an untouchable phantom, but a battered young man needing to be rescued.

A series of gunshots downstairs jolted her from her thoughts. She knelt and sliced the zip ties securing the hacker's wrists behind his back. "We need to move," she said, slipping an arm around his back and under his right shoulder. "Can you walk?"

"Where are we?" he said, his voice dry and raspy.

"Cape Town. Come on. We need to—"

"I can't go anywhere," he said, catching her off guard. "I'm staying right here." His legs gave out, and he dropped back to the floor, taking her with him until she let go of him.

"What the hell are you doing?" Alejandra said, dropping and wrapping her arm around him again.

"I can't go anywhere." He coughed and bowed his head. "He'll kill us all if I leave. He told me so, again and again. I'm staying here."

"Are you crazy? This maniac will try and kill us all anyway. You really want to follow his orders?"

Murph paused and looked away. "You don't know him like I do. None of you do. You don't know what he's capable of. He knew you'd all come. It was a ruse. All part of his plan. His twisted game."

"Yeah, we figured that much out."

Murph shook his head. "And you came anyway?"

"Yeah, we damn well came anyway. What, you expect us to back off and be scared of this lunatic just because he's got a plan? Screw his plan. We're not afraid of him, Murph, and you shouldn't be, either."

The hacker hunched farther toward the floor and closed his eyes. "You don't know what he's capable of."

"I don't care. We're going to stop him, or we're going to die trying. But we're not gonna sit on the sidelines while he winds his little webs."

Murph shuddered and swallowed hard, then looked her in the eyes. "This is Cipher we're talking about."

She knelt beside him. "Yeah, and you're Murph. You're better than he is, you hear me?"

"He captured me."

"Yeah, and I just rescued you. Who cares? You're gonna win in the end because you're better than he is."

"There's nothing that can be done. It's too late."

"There's always something that can be done. And you're gonna figure it out because you're better than he is."

"Why do you keep saying that?"

"Because it's true. And you're about to prove it. Now, get on your feet and problem-solve and figure this out. The whole world's counting on you."

THIRTY-ONE

AGENT ROYAL INCHED along the ledge and entered the castle through the second-floor window. Once inside the hallway, she retrieved her service pistol and listened carefully. There were no sounds aside from the music screaming from the outdoor speakers and the occasional gunshot downstairs.

Her only mission being to get to Cipher as quickly as possible, she crept to the end of the hall, then rounded a corner. Remembering the schematics, she knew the doorway to the upper-level walkway leading to the base of the tower was just ahead of her to the right.

Royal made it two quick steps down the hall when a door slammed open in front of her, and a wide-shouldered man in a bulletproof vest stomped out. He was talking into his earpiece radio but froze when he saw her.

"Hands in the air," Royal ordered, aiming her pistol at him.

The man glared and took a step toward her.

"I said hands up!" she shouted.

He ignored her and charged. She opened fire, exploding a 9mm round into his chest. He grunted from the forceful blow but kept coming, closing the distance, snatching her by the wrist, and wrestling the weapon free while she fired twice more into the ceiling. The pistol fell to the floor, and he smacked her face, whirling her into a one-eighty and sending her into the wall.

The man stood tall and pressed a hand to the bullet lodged deep into his Kevlar.

He snarled and stomped toward her again, trying to grab her from behind. She ducked, then sprang skyward, pounding an elbow up into his jaw. He snapped backward, and before he could recover, the CIA operative spun and landed a powerful roundhouse that sent the guard flying into the nearby window. The glass shattered, and he broke through, yelling wildly as he flailed and spun, smacking into a path far below.

Royal peered through the newly formed opening in the heart of the window and saw movement. She stepped forward and spotted a hooded figure standing at the top of the tower. He was moving stuff around, then took post along the opposite wall.

Knowing it was Cipher, she took off down the hall and hustled along the walkway into the turret. She reached a narrow staircase and wasted no time taking on the steps that spiraled up the tower in complete darkness. After completing a revolution, footsteps echoed up the staircase.

She picked up her pace, then heard footsteps coming from above, as well. Royal took aim but couldn't see anything in either direction. Both sounds grew louder, closing in before stopping in unison.

Royal kneeled and aimed back and forth, trying to stay as quiet as possible. She couldn't wait forever, so she made a choice. Aiming ahead, she rushed up the stairs, but before she even made it two steps, a blinding light washed over her, the intense beam forcing her to turn her head and shut her eyes.

Boots stomped from below, and strong arms grabbed her in the confusion. She opened fire but was swiftly lifted up, her weapon ripped from her hands. She thrashed and screamed at the top of her lungs, the sounds amplified in the confined space. A blunt object smacked against her head, nearly knocking her unconscious and sending her into a daze.

"I want her kept alert," a Russian voice said.

The strong arms heaved her off the ground as if she weighed nothing and carried her up the rest of the way. She was brought into a confined room, and the men forced her into a chair, her head swaying back and forth.

A face appeared, pale as snow with chilling gray eyes.

"Hello, Agent Royal," Cipher said.

She could barely hold a thought as she struggled to stave off unconsciousness, let alone formulate a response.

Cipher smiled, then stood tall and eyed his men. "We've lured one guest into the tower. Now it's time to lure a second."

THIRTY-TWO

THE LIGHTS FLICKED out when Jason reached the top of the stairs. The music was still pounding, pulsating the walls and blaring obnoxiously. Three gunshots fired in rapid succession, all of them coming from behind the door at the far end of the hall in front of him.

Jason knew it had to be Alejandra. He pushed forward, his pistol clutched in his hand. Pain screamed from all over his body, and he was wobbly from the scuffle with the assassin. He'd faced off against formidable opponents before, and the guy had been as tough as any he'd fought—experienced and precise and strong as an ox. Jason had made it out, but he felt the effects of the encounter.

The pain and dizziness weren't going to stop him from finding and engaging Cipher. Halfway down the hall, he came to the upper-level walkway extending toward the tower. He moved around the corner and out onto the narrow path, then rushed across as quickly as he could.

He cut under an eave and reached another staircase. Its revolutions were tighter and only led up. Jason raised his weapon, taking each step slowly and quietly while listening for any movement. The stairway eventually ended at a door that was propped open. He peeked inside, his aim following his every glance. The room was dark aside from a monitor screen and an outside light entering through one window. A short wooden ladder hinged down, leading to an open hatch overhead.

Cipher stood in the middle, his body half facing Jason, but his eyes on the monitor. He appeared unarmed but held something small in his right hand.

"Freeze, Cipher!" Jason pointed his weapon at the notorious criminal. "Hands in the air."

The man remained still as stone, his eyes glued to the screen. The monitor displayed a light gray color and a faint series of numbers in the corner of the screen.

"Come on in, Jason Wake." His words were slow and casual. "The show's just about to begin."

"I said hands in the air, now!"

He was moments away from putting a bullet through Cipher's knee when the criminal held up his right hand, revealing a square device, his thumb pressing down on a red button in the center.

"Not so fast, Wake. You take another step, and I'll blow this entire place sky high." He gazed through the wall in the direction of the parking lot. "By the looks of it, there are at least two dozen US and South African agents on site. If you shoot me, I'll let go."

Jason took a step into the room. He heard shuffling beside him and turned, but not fast enough. A tall, muscular guard smacked him in the hands with a baton, nearly cracking his wrist and sending his pistol tumbling to the floor. A second guard appeared, grabbing Jason from behind and kicking the back of his left leg. It gave out beneath his weight, and his two-hundred-pound frame collapsed forward.

Jason turned to retaliate, only to find the barrels of two high-caliber pistols aimed at his head.

Cipher motioned toward a chair. "Have a seat, Wake."

The two guards grabbed Jason forcefully and shoved him into the chair.

Cipher faced Jason. "You know, you continue to surprise me and exceed my expectations. Axe has been my go-to asset for target elimination. He's one of the finest assassins in the world."

"*Was* one of the finest assassins in the world," Jason said. "But drawing swords against me was a big mistake—the last he'll ever make."

Cipher laughed sadistically. "Well, then, he's not the only one to make a fatal, life-altering mistake tonight. I'm afraid you've underestimated me, as well." He looked out the open window at the meteor shower. "Incredible, isn't it?"

Jason said nothing.

"As I said, you've arrived just in time for the show. But not this show." Cipher waved a hand at the sky. "No, there's something even more special that's about to begin. In fact"—he checked his watch—"yes, I think this is the perfect time."

Using his left hand, he clicked a button on a remote, and the screen flashed from light gray to a quick frame of static to a distinct image in a light-green hue.

Jason focused on the live picture of a wide stretch of water flanked by desert. In the middle of the waterway was a container ship. The camera was far off, but the vessel was clearly fully loaded. Jason squinted to read the words on the side of the ship, but he couldn't make them out.

"She's the *SS Cyclops*," Cipher said. "One of the largest moving objects ever created by man. One of the pride and joys of the United States' commercial transport fleet." He smiled, then checked his watch again. "Just out of curiosity . . . Did you ever learn how many cruise missiles were stolen from the Iranian weapons facility?"

Jason thought back to his last talk with Murph. When the number jumped into his mind, his blood boiled.

Two, he thought.

Cipher smiled when the realization showed in Jason's eyes. "Why do you think I lured you and your team here to the bottom of Africa? I needed you out of the picture to make sure this last piece of the puzzle fit snug." He checked his watch a final time, then held up his left index finger as he watched the screen. "And here . . . we . . . go."

He snapped his fingers, and an object appeared, screaming into frame on the right side of the picture, flashing across in a blur of white, and then blasting into the container ship. The rocket struck the aft section of the vessel just above the waterline, and a massive explosion burst out, blinding the feed for a moment. The vessel blew apart like an erupting volcano, consumed by the intense force. The ship was covered in a monster of flames and smoke. One moment it was there, and the next, completely destroyed.

THIRTY-THREE

SCOTT COOPER WAS no stranger to infiltrating enemy compounds. He had no trouble sneaking past the remaining guards outside the castle, the former Navy SEAL commander integrating with the throngs of scattering partygoers as he headed for the side door. He slipped into the ballroom, acting natural as he headed toward the main hall.

On the way, he noticed a canister resting on the black-and-white checkered floor. He crouched down and realized it was a flash grenade—a nasty little bugger he'd been on the receiving end of more than once. The grenade emitted a blinding flash at a staggering intensity of roughly seven megacandela.

Scott removed his pistol when he reached the main hallway, picking up the pace as he headed for the stairs. Following the schematic, he stepped into the bowels of the medieval structure. The air cooled as he entered another hall, this one underground and with a far shorter overhead. A wine cellar was off to the right, and a food storage area was beside it. Water tanks for the catchment system and webs of piping covered the area to his left.

He came to a metal cage that ran floor to ceiling and took up an entire back corner. Scott eyed a big padlock on the gate, then slid off his backpack and unzipped the main compartment. He'd brought three small charges of C4, each rigged separately and detonable with his phone.

Grabbing one of the charges, he planted it on the padlock and took cover, blowing the charge and blasting the lock and door away. He waited and listened—doubting anyone above would even notice the noise with the music and screaming people outside.

Stepping out from his cover, he tossed aside the partially unhinged gate and stepped through to a monstrous machine. Hovering his hand over the generator's controls, he clicked the manual shutoff and locked it in place, then he cracked open a circuit breaker box on the wall.

Like many facilities and mansions, he expected the power to operate with a relay backup power switching circuit, causing the generator to kick on and power the place in the event of a loss of city power. Tracing a hand over the inside of the box, he located and clicked open the main breaker, and the power in the castle went out. With the generator manually shut down, there was no alternate power source to rely upon.

He listened for any of Cipher's men sent down to investigate. When no one came, he stepped back through the remnants of the charred gate and down the hall, wanting to reach the tower and help the others take down Cipher as quickly as possible.

Scott passed the water tanks and piping before moving beside a long dark space next to the wine cellar. He cut back two strides, clicked on his flashlight, and angled his head for a better look. In the corner of a storage area, among pillars of stacked chairs and tables, were three large barrels resting against each other. Set on top of the barrels was a rectangular metal device with wires branching out of it and into the barrels.

Eyeing the heavy explosives, he swallowed hard, then withdrew his knife and approached them slowly.

THIRTY-FOUR

JASON WATCHED IN horror, his hands tightening into shaky fists. He couldn't believe what he was seeing.

Cipher let out a breath and fell into a chair beside Jason. He watched the wreckage rain down across the water, the flames settle to intense orbs concentrated near the fuel tanks, and the smoke begin to clear.

"Forgive me, Wake, but sometimes, being a mastermind takes a lot out of you."

"Go to hell," Jason grunted through his teeth.

Cipher laughed and then sauntered to the screen. He pointed at the burning remnants of the vessel. "You're only angry at yourself because you've failed. Despite all of your team's efforts, you couldn't succeed. You couldn't beat me." He chuckled again. "You should've listened to Murph. He warned you. I know he did."

The vile criminal gazed at the screen again. "And so, the final part of the plan has come to fruition. The dominoes are falling one by one, and they will continue to fall. There's nothing you can do to stop it now. The world will go to war . . . again. There's no other outcome. Not after this."

"You're going to pay for everything you've done," Jason snapped.

Cipher watched as a meteor poked out of the heavens and into our atmosphere, watching as it burned up and fizzled out in a brilliant streak.

"Maybe so, Wake. Maybe so. But not tonight. And not by you."

He stepped closer to the window, then turned to one of his men. "Time for the finale."

The guy nodded, then made a call.

Jason pulled with all his strength at the thick plastic securing his wrists together, the zip ties digging into his flesh as his arms shook.

The guy said a few mumbled words into his phone, then hung up and gestured to Cipher.

The criminal planted his hands on his hips and stared out the open window. "Feast your eyes, Wake."

A moment after the words left his lips, a chorus of explosions filled the air. Dozens of fireworks left thick streams of sparkling dust in their wakes, and rockets burst in a powerful, colorful flurry of blinding light. In the heart of the explosions, a dark object, suspended in the air, was struck and spun out of control before whining toward the earth.

Cipher laughed, watching as the object fell out of the sky and smashed into the hillside to the south. "You think we didn't know about your little drone?"

More fireworks exploded, then Cipher gestured to one of the guards.

The guy made another call, then said, "Everything's ready, sir."

Cipher slung a backpack over his shoulder, then gave Jason a mock salute with his right hand, which was still holding down the red button.

"Alas, it's time to bid adieu." He leaned down and looked Jason in the eyes. "You really did surprise me, you know. You should feel good about that." He patted Jason on the shoulder. "You made a good effort. And you made this whole endeavor all the more enjoyable for me. The hardest earned victories taste sweetest, don't you agree? Now, if you'll excuse me, I have some money to count." A sadistic chuckle escaped his lips, then he stepped toward the middle of the room.

Grabbing the base of the ladder leading to the top of the tower, he turned to Jason one more time. "Oh, and don't you or anyone else even think of chasing after us. We've got a little extra insurance with us, just in case."

The criminal motioned skyward, and one of his men forced Agent Royal into Jason's view. She was tied up and gagged, and her eyes were terror-struck.

Cipher gave another mock salute and smiled. "Until next time, Jason Wake."

He only made it one step up the ladder before a loud boom shook the space.

The heavy locked door to the stairwell splintered off its hinges and blasted to pieces in a powerful shockwave.

"Get down!" One of the guards lifted the metal table and used it as a shield.

Gunfire cracked, and one of the guards was struck in the side. The other returned fire, sending streams of rounds down the stairwell.

While Cipher was momentarily distracted by the shots, Jason lunged forward, his bound hands reaching for the button tucked in the criminal's right palm. Cipher tried to jerk him away, but Jason was bigger and stronger and managed to tear the device free while keeping the button held down. But the act left Jason fully exposed, and Cipher grinned maniacally as he withdrew a six-inch blade and stabbed it at Jason.

The tip tore through the Kevlar, the blade barely piercing Jason's flesh. Cipher's eyes widened in surprise, and before he could yank the knife free for another blow, Jason snapped his head forward, bashing his forehead into the side of the criminal's face.

The scrawny hacker lurched back as the second guard appeared, grabbing Jason from behind and hurtling him into the wall. The blow nearly knocked Jason unconscious, and he fell to the stone floor, the loosely gripped detonator flying from his hand.

With the button no longer depressed, Jason and Cipher stared at the device, watching in horror as it clattered against the floor.

But no explosion followed.

Gunfire erupted from the stairwell once more. Cipher sprang for the ladder and climbed away from the bullets whizzing by and blasting into the walls. The guard followed right behind but was struck in the leg by a round, slowing him for a second before he continued his escape behind Cipher. The two vanished onto the roof of the tower, then slammed shut the thick hatch behind them.

In the confusion of the gunfight, Jason crawled behind the cover of the upturned metal table. "Don't shoot!" He winced as he dug the knife out from the Kevlar and his chest. Using the razor-sharp edge, he slashed the zip tie off his wrists.

Scott appeared with his pistol raised and scanned the room before his gaze rested on Jason. The covert operative was already breaking for the ladder. No words were exchanged as he threw himself up the rungs and then shoved himself against the bottom of the hatch. The thick slab of oak wouldn't give.

Scott removed a charge of C4. "Get back!"

Jason jumped aside, and the former Navy SEAL commander stuck the explosive to the corner of the hatch. They cleared back into the stairwell, and when they were out of harm's way, Scott blew the charge, the sharp explosion shaking the turret.

Jason led the way back up and brushed away a thin veil of smoke to see the hatch blown halfway off the frame, offering plenty of room to squeeze through. With the ladder also blown away, he leapt, grabbed the edges of stone, and heaved himself onto the top of the tower.

There was no sign of Cipher or his guards. As Scott climbed behind him, Jason spotted a bazooka-shaped device on the ground. Stepping to the edge of the turret, he also saw a long cable secured around one of the merlons and reaching far out to the north, into the shadows along the slope of the nearby mountainside.

Scott approached, and Jason removed his holster, needing something he could use to slide down the zipline. Cars were thundering into the parking lot—a backup team consisting of dozens of armed soldiers and government agents. But none of them were close enough to have seen Cipher and his guards make the daring escape.

Just as Jason removed his holster and was about to wrap it around the cable, the line went loose in an instant, the other end snapping free and the metal rope dropping lifelessly and coming to rest against the steep wall of the spire.

Seeing far-off, shadowy figures escaping through the dense growth up the hillside, Jason climbed over the side and grabbed hold of the cable. He wrapped the strong nylon part of his holster around the line. "I'm going after him, Scottie. You gotta figure out who hired him. It's all for nothing if we don't."

Jason kicked off and rappelled, sliding down the cable and using the fabric to protect his hand. He hit the ground harder than he'd hoped, bending his legs to absorb the impact as best as he could. His left hand burned as he released the holster and took off across the northern part of the compound.

THIRTY-FIVE

"**You need to** think, Murph," Alejandra said, trying to snap the hacker out of it and get him to take action. "There has to be a way."

"There isn't. Cipher keeps everything secured. Locked tight. You heard of Fort Knox?"

"Fort Knox isn't impenetrable."

The brilliant but defeated hacker closed his eyes a moment, then looked up. "Even if it were possible, I'd need my computer."

A muffled explosion shuddered the castle just enough to chime the chandelier overhead. It was followed immediately by the chaotic sounds of sporadic gunshots coming from the direction of the tower.

Alejandra stared toward the noises, then held out a hand to Murph. "We've got you covered, Murph. Now, come on."

She clasped his hand and heaved him to his feet, leading him toward the entryway. Still gripping her pistol, she listened through the door and then opened it just enough to see the entire length of the hallway. It was empty, and through the lines of windows, she saw the tower just across from them.

She stepped out and motioned for Murph to follow. The hacker was far out of his element but did his best to keep calm. The past twelve hours had been a severe mind game—a test unlike any he'd been put through before. He'd been blindfolded nearly every second of it and struck and bombarded with threats that led him to accept he'd likely be offed at any second.

Alejandra led him to the doorway off the hallway, then turned onto the bridge extending to the base of the tower. They made it two steps when they saw movement coming from the top.

"Get down," she said, then took aim.

But a second after Cipher appeared, so did a tied-up Agent Royal, carried by a massive guard, the agent blocking most of Alejandra's shot. Then the three vanished from view, moving to the opposite side of the spire.

"Come on," Alejandra gasped, and they took off across the walkway.

A second explosion came from the tower, causing them to freeze before taking on the spiral staircase. They wound around three times before reaching a battered door and a cramped room. Alejandra scanned it with her pistol, then she heard Jason and Scott, their voices emanating through an open hatch in the ceiling.

She called out to them, then Scott appeared and climbed down.

"Cipher?" Alejandra said.

"He's on the run." Scott looked over his operative and Murph, then placed a hand on the hacker's shoulder. "I'm glad to see you in one piece, Murph." The covert leader grabbed his backpack off the floor, and seeing that Murph was flustered and terrified, looked deep into the hacker's eyes, displaying supreme confidence. "There comes a time in everyone's life when they face an ultimate challenge—one that puts all their abilities to the greatest test." He held the backpack out to Murph. "This is that moment. There's no better man alive for this job than you. You can do this."

Scott unzipped the main compartment, revealing a stowed laptop and other hacking essentials Murph had developed.

Murph slid out the computer. It was an advanced, top-of-the-line model that was even better than the one he typically used. The best computing firepower money could buy.

Murph looked around at the nearly empty space. It was clear that Cipher had taken his electronics with him. The renowned criminal mastermind had left no trace of his online activities behind—nothing that could be used to figure out who'd hired him.

Murph stepped across the room and looked around more thoroughly, poking his head under the chairs and table and running through the shelves of medieval literature. One of the books was an old, faded edition of *Snow White and the Seven Dwarfs*. The cover faced forward and rested on a brass stand. That version of the book had sketches on the cover, the scene flanked by the shape of the magic mirror.

Murph stared at the cover, transfixed by the magic mirror that offered the answer to any question. The hacker gazed back at the monitor's black screen.

Maybe Cipher didn't remember everything.

He stepped across the room, checked the monitor's make and model, the ports and power plug, and then spotted an HDMI cable resting in the shadows. He scooped it up and checked both ends.

"I might have something." He debated with himself, trying to reason his way through the task at hand. "It's beyond far-fetched . . . but it's possible."

THIRTY-SIX

JASON BOLTED ACROSS the corner of the property and shouldered his way through the gate just as the horde of vehicles thundered up behind him, their sirens blaring.

He cut out to a dirt path and charged along the side of the mountain as fast as he could, heading toward the shadowy figures he'd spotted in the brush.

He ran along for what felt like ages. His body was exhausted and aching from the rough encounters at the castle, but all he could think about was Marcus, Agent Royal, and the recent footage of the American container ship being blown to pieces in the Middle East.

The bomb strike meant his efforts could all be in vain—that Cipher could very well be right, and that

America was going to war regardless of what happened next or what Jason and his team were able to prove. The dominos were falling . . .

He shoved the thoughts aside with a powerful mental hook, prodding his focus to the task at hand. Cresting a steep rise, he stopped to catch his breath and listen.

He heard nothing and wondered if he'd gone the wrong way or gotten turned around in the darkness. He gazed back toward the castle below, the grounds swarming with officers and blinding against the dark backdrop. He created a mental line from the top of the tower to where the end of the cable had been attached.

After convincing himself he was heading in the right direction, he turned and nearly ran into a short metal spear sticking out of the base of a tree trunk. A foot of frayed cable dangled on the end of it.

He pressed on into the night, pumping his arms and driving his legs. He weaved through the thick foliage until he heard the unmistakable sound of an internal combustion engine, followed by the acceleration of rotors.

Jason veered off the path, following a winding break in the brush. The growth dissipated, revealing a helicopter swiftly warming up. It was tucked along a steep slope of rock. A pile of camouflage tarps and netting beside it had clearly been used to conceal the aircraft.

Jason popped out just as Royal was forced inside, her mouth still gagged and hands still secured as she was heaved into the cabin. Cipher climbed in next, and then the remaining guard.

Jason skirted along the clearing, then took off, sprinting toward the tail. The cabin door shut, and the main rotor accelerated more. The engine whined, and the skids lifted off the dirt. Pebbles and dust swirled underneath, pelting into Jason as he pushed forward.

Just as the helicopter rose off the ground, Jason jumped and caught the left skid. The craft tilted slightly on his landing, and he held on as the vehicle rapidly soared into the sky. The engine and rotors were deafening, the wind howling like it was trying to force him off. The helicopter ascended to three hundred feet, then thundered over the mountainside, flying over the peaks and revealing the bright city lights of Cape Town.

The pilot swept northeast, turning enough for the outline of the imposing and uniquely shaped Table Mountain to come into view off the craft's right side. Jason held on as the world blurred past beneath his dangling feet. He pulled himself up and planted his right heel onto the steel bar.

The craft turned sharply just as he got his footing, whipping his momentum around and nearly jostling him off. He gripped tight, gritting his teeth, and forcing his muscles to work in overdrive as he regained control and inched toward the cabin door. He was crouched down, just beneath the view of the rear windows. The door was ahead of him, the handle six inches from his outstretched fingers.

As he reached for the door, it suddenly cracked open, and a hand holding a pistol appeared. In a daring effort to escape the path of the weapon's aim, Jason let go of the skid with his right hand, twisted around and jumped, sliding headfirst along the landing gear just as rounds burst from the pistol.

With the bullets flashing from the chamber, Jason caught himself on the forward crossbar, his shoulder slamming into the metal and his body nearly falling again. With the pistol still aimed out the door and its wielder adjusting his position, Jason threw himself into the door from the opposite side, slamming hard and smashing it against his adversary's forearm. The bone cracked, the sound muffled by the chomping rotors and rushing wind. The pistol fell free, rattling against the landing gear before spinning out of sight in a free fall toward the barren landscape below.

Jason caught his first glimpse of his attacker through the window and saw that it was Cipher. Wanting to land another blow as quickly as possible, Jason swung back and grabbed the handle. But by the time he'd completed the maneuver and forced the door open against the gusts, Cipher had vanished to the other side of the cabin and the guard had taken his place.

With both of Jason's hands busy holding himself to the side of the moving aircraft, the man lurched forward and wrapped his meaty hands around Jason's exposed neck. He jerked Jason forward and forced him outward. Jason let go with his right hand and tried to attack the guy, but there was only the tight opening between the door and the frame, and Jason couldn't reach him.

Needing to make a last-ditch effort, Jason arched down his chin and used his right hand to force one of the guy's thumbs between his teeth. Jason chomped down, cracking the bone like a carrot. The guy yelled out and loosened his grip, and Jason used the momentary lapse to stab a thumb into the guy's left eye.

The man yelled louder, and before he could retaliate, Jason shifted free, grabbed him by his shirt collar, then swung left and muscled the man out of the cabin. He fell halfway out before catching himself on the outer frame. He reached for Jason again but was met by a solid kick to the forehead. He tumbled headfirst, battering along the fuselage before soaring out. His lower body struck the tail rotor and severed brutally before he vanished into the night.

The helicopter shook as the tail rotor sputtered and smoked. They turned sharply right, the force pinning Jason against the outer window as they soared toward the steep cliffs of Table Mountain. As the rock faces flew past beside them, Jason forced the door open again and climbed inside. Upon entering the cabin, he looked up to Cipher on the other side of the seat. Royal was in front of him, gagged and tied, with a pistol pressed to her temple.

"An impressive effort, Wake, but it's over."

The criminal mastermind jerked Royal tight, then angled the weapon at Jason. As he did, the CIA operative threw the back of her head into his face. He grunted from the unexpected blow, and his body twisted, his gun hand arcing with the sudden shudder. He opened fire, blasting a round that tore through the seat in front of them and drove into the pilot's chest.

The pilot shook, and the aircraft jerked wildly, cutting right and soaring back, nearly striking the towering rock walls beside them.

Jason pounced moments after the shot was fired, throwing himself across the seat toward Cipher. The helicopter jerked left, tilting to a dangerously sharp angle and sending Jason flying backward against the door frame. He caught himself and could only watch as Royal and Cipher went at it, the government agent fighting for control of the criminal's pistol.

The helicopter turned sharply back again, the pilot gagging and shaking as they descended toward the city and skyscrapers. They weaved between buildings in a blur, descending toward the waterfront like one of the distant meteors.

Jason climbed back across the seat and landed two punches to Cipher's head. The hacker lurched back in a daze and loosened his grip. Jason knocked his pistol free and pulled Royal loose, then punched Cipher again, this time in the chest. The scrawny hacker heaved and struggled for air.

"Who hired you?" Jason roared.

The back-to-back series of events made Jason furious to a level he'd never been before.

Cipher spat and said nothing, so Jason punched the criminal again, bashing his knuckles across his face.

"Who?" Jason yelled.

The helicopter tilted again, and Jason and Royal held on. A glance through the windshield told Jason they'd descended even more. Buildings flew past, most of them towering over them as they shook toward the downtown harbor.

"I'll never tell you, Wake. There's nothing you can do."

Jason withdrew his knife—the same one Cipher stabbed him with at the castle—and drove it down into the hacker's left thigh. The blade pierced deep, and Cipher screamed like mad.

"There's . . . nothing you can do, Wake!"

The helicopter dropped down under a hundred feet, then flew over the waterfront and the lines of tourists and restaurants at the harbor's edge.

The craft jolted again as Jason twisted the blade to increase the pain. The helicopter tilted abruptly, and Jason tumbled back, keeping the knife firm in his grasp and pulling it free as the door swung open behind him and Royal.

Enraged, Cipher shifted his position, planted his back against the opposite door, and kicked with his right leg, jamming his heel into Jason and knocking him backward. The chopper angled even sharper, and Jason and Royal tumbled out the open door, soaring toward the water below.

THIRTY-SEVEN

MURPH TURNED TO face Scott and Alejandra, then pointed at the screen. "That's a smart monitor, and I'm willing to bet that Cipher's laptop was hooked up to it when the power shut off."

Neither Scott nor Alejandra understood the significance or where he was going with that. "When it boots back up," Murph said, more to himself than the others, "there will be a brief flash of memory—a small stream of data stored and trying to regain the previous connection. Every interaction online involves back-and-forth transactions between servers. Each session between computers and remote servers is given a unique session ID, and it's that ID that should still be stored in the monitor as RAM."

It was way over their heads—a level of hacking know-how that only a handful of people had ever reached.

Murph tapped a finger against his bottom lip. "With the power going out when it did, and with the attack and Cipher's rushed escape, I'm betting he didn't have enough time to properly clear the monitor . . . or even think about it."

"He also planned to blow this whole place," Scott said. "I may have stumbled upon some explosives in the basement."

Seeing that Murph's mind was hard at work, Scott and Alejandra fell silent, not wanting to risk derailing the man from his current train of thought. They didn't need to understand what he was talking about or what he was trying to do. The explanation could come later.

After another minute of internal chatter, Murph turned to them. "This might be possible."

Scott nodded. "If anyone can do it, it's you. What do you need, Murph?"

"Solitude and silence . . . and caffeine, if possible. And I'll need the power switched back on when I give the signal."

Scott reached into the backpack and pulled out an energy drink—a cylinder packed with over fifty grams of sugar and three hundred milligrams of caffeine. Then he and Alejandra backed away and lifted the damaged door.

They both shot Murph a look.

"I'll let you know when I'm in position," Scott said as they shuffled out and snugged the door into place behind them.

Murph cracked open the laptop and booted it up. Popping open the soda can, he splashed half its contents down his parched throat, instantly feeling the rush as the cool liquid flowed into his stomach.

When the computer was up and running, he clicked open three different programs and arranged them so they were all visible at once. He closed his eyes and breathed slowly in and out, clearing his mind.

He took another long sip of his drink then closed his eyes again, visualizing what he'd need to do. After a minute, he practiced typing and navigating the different programs using a blistering series of shortcut inputs, shortening the gap between his mind, body, and the machine. Microseconds were an eternity in his world, and any mistake—however minute—and any hesitation—no matter how minuscule—would cost him the hack. It would cost all of them the entire mission.

He set the can down and focused intensely.

Scott's voice crackled through the radio. "In position, Murph."

Murph leaned forward and connected the HDMI cable to his laptop. He felt the pressure of the moment intensify with the act and the weight of the mission on his shoulders. Operating under stressful, high-stakes conditions with innocent lives on the line had never gotten to him before. He'd always been focused and even clutch under the direst of circumstances.

Being bested and captured by Cipher was a powerful blow, but Alejandra's words popped into his mind. She and Scott were unwaveringly confident in their belief in his abilities. He'd been bested, sure, but that didn't make him less than Cipher. He reminded himself of the hundreds of times he'd pushed through and succeeded against overwhelming odds—that he'd done the impossible.

He could do it again. And he would do it again.

"On three, Scott," he said, the words flowing out of his mouth unconsciously. "Three . . . two . . . one . . . execute."

The world fell away completely, and he could almost feel the whir of electricity, the flow of electrons as the negatively charged subatomic particles tore through the conductor.

The screen powered on, and a nearly instantaneous flash of intel appeared on one of the programs running on Murph's laptop. With lightning-quick reflexes, Murph caught the data stream, middle-manned the latest transaction, re-triggered the session, and hijacked the monitor's ID, all in less than two seconds before the data expired.

With the necessary intel captured, he brought up a clone connection under the previous session ID. The first part had been beyond difficult given the minuscule window of opportunity, but the second aspect of the ploy rested on a wing and a prayer.

The code streamed across his screen, then paused, then connected for a brief moment and flashed with the server's details. Once again, Murph managed to extract the session identity and its recently connected IPs. The connection severed, flagged as expired less than a second after he'd entered, then the data stream vanished. But Murph had already transferred everything over to his device in a swift maneuver, the muscle memory dexterity of which amazed even himself.

He gasped out a breath and sucked in air for the first time in what felt like ages. Staying in the zone, he scanned the intel he'd managed to secure, hoping to find something, anything that could point to whoever Cipher was working with.

He didn't have to search for long. Among the lines of encrypted code, he uncovered an IP address. His eyes lit up as he ran a quick search for the address, then he leaned back as the device and its registered owner's name appeared on his screen.

THIRTY-EIGHT

JASON AND ROYAL spun wildly, feeling the wind gust faster and faster by them. They free-fell fifty feet and then splashed into the harbor, the sixty-degree water biting at their skin as they were enveloped in darkness. Following the collision, everything went silent, then bubbles gurgled past in a haze and raced for the surface.

Jason had let go of Royal, mid-air, not wanting to slam into her in the confusion. He opened his eyes briefly, just long enough to see a blur of the CIA agent kicking for the surface. Jason did the same, and the two broke free nearly at the same time.

The rush from the cold caused their breathing to quicken and their eyes to broaden as they wiped away the water and brushed aside their hair. Their gazes were locked to the west as the helicopter continued its chaotic, sputtering, uncontrolled descent. The engine squealed and protested, and a stream of black smoke spewed from its damaged tail.

They watched as the craft covered a quarter mile, nearly reaching the main entrance into the harbor, then shook and tilted into a nosedive, crashing into the water.

The fuel tank blew, and flashes of fire enveloped the wreckage. They mushroomed at first, then steadied to an inferno as a burst of smoke rose into the sky. The burning remnants sank, and the flames finally fizzled, the heat congregating around the floating fuel.

Shaking from the cold, Royal treaded water beside Jason, then kicked over to him and threw her arms around him, squeezing tight. After a brief moment, they broke apart and swam for a nearby floating dock with a metal ladder.

Royal climbed up before Jason, and once they ascended, they rushed down a walkway. They both shivered as the ocean air brushed against their soaked bodies. On the promenade ahead of them were lines of curious spectators staring out over the harbor at the smoking helicopter. Behind them were lines of two-story restaurants, packed nearly full and lit up. The whole downtown area was immaculate and full of life, and all eyes were on them as they headed up a ramp to the boardwalk.

Jason was about to ask to borrow someone's phone when the sound of boat engines hijacked his thoughts. Royal was already watching as a blacked-out RHIB cut into view near the mouth of the harbor.

For a moment, they thought it might be the South African Coast Guard or a good Samaritan searching for survivors, but the boat cruised past the downed aircraft, motoring in their direction two hundred yards, then idling. Jason stepped to the edge and watched as a man heaved himself out of the waterway and was helped up into the boat.

"You've got to be kidding me," Royal gasped,

Jason could nearly hear her heart breaking.

They both knew who it was, and they could only watch from a quarter mile away as the criminal mastermind settled into the boat and the engines fired back up, rocketing the vessel back toward the mouth of the harbor. As the boat passed the remaining cluster of fire, the light splashed over the occupants, and Jason caught a flash of Cipher standing at the stern and staring back at them.

He knew what the murderer would be thinking, and the same sentiment occupied Jason's thoughts.

This isn't over.

Jason and Royal turned around as two waterfront security guards ran toward them, both wearing white uniforms with blue vests and matching hats. One of them held a stack of emergency blankets, and the other had a first aid kit.

"Are you all right?" one guard said.

They assured the guards they were fine, and they were each handed a blanket. Jason unraveled his and draped it over Royal.

"What the hell happened?" the other guard said.

Jason ignored the question and asked to borrow his phone. He stepped away from the two guards, and Scott picked up on the first ring.

"Cipher got away, Scottie. He's on a boat racing away from the V&A waterfront harbor. If we—"

"We don't need him, Jase. Murph figured it out." Jason shot a relieved look toward Royal, then Scott added, "You two sit tight. We'll meet you downtown along the main drag."

After hanging up, Jason motioned for Royal to follow him inland, but the CIA agent stood her ground.

"You're going after Cipher?" Jason said, reading her body language.

She glared toward the mouth of the harbor as the boat motored out of view. "He's the one I'm after, Jason."

They exchanged a brief, knowing look, then Royal peeled away, slipping out her phone and calling one of her local contacts. As they split up, Jason realized that she'd never told him why catching Cipher was so important to her. Why she'd had strong personal motives for hunting down the criminal mastermind long before her partner had been killed.

Fifteen minutes later, Jason cut through the waterfront restaurants and shops and stood beside the Cape Ferris Wheel as a black Suburban braked along the road. Alejandra was in the front seat, and Finn and Murph in the middle, so he slid into the back, and Scott hit the gas.

"Good to meet you in person, finally," Jason said, extending a hand to Murph. "I knew you'd find a way."

The hacker smiled, then Scott said, "What happened to the helicopter?"

"It had a little engine trouble. And pilot trouble." Jason rubbed his chin. "Cipher must've had guys in position. He must've been planning to fly to the waterfront, though probably not with such an explosive landing. He had to have jumped for it just before the bird crashed."

"At least it wasn't all in vain, thanks to Murph," Alejandra said, tapping his shoulder.

"The wizard pulled it off," Scott said. "But we've got another problem . . . A big one."

THIRTY-NINE

SCOTT ROARED THEM away from the waterfront, weaving in and out of the busy downtown streets.

"Long story short," Murph explained, "I was able to figure out not only the server Cipher connected with while livestreaming the missile strike on the container ship in the Gulf of Hormuz, but also the IP of another computer linked to the feed. My hope was that whoever hired him was also watching the attack—you know, to prove that Cipher was following through on the deal, and as some form of sick satisfaction on the buyer's part."

"So, you were able to track them down because Cipher set up the monitor for me to watch it live?" Jason said. "More than a little ironic."

Murph nodded. "The IP address was linked to a computer registered by a Chinese corporation called Lotus Global. I'm somewhat familiar with the mysterious company. They have a reputation for unethical international business dealings, though nothing's ever been formally laid against them. The CEO is a man named Ru Xiang, a hard-charging guy barely in his forties, who's made a name for himself in finance and global politics."

"You think he's our guy?" Jason said.

"It's possible, but no, I don't. I think this is our guy."

He angled the laptop so Jason could see a grainy photograph of a gray-haired Chinese man wearing a black suit. He was surrounded by bodyguards, the zoomed-in picture barely able to make out most of his face.

"Who is he?"

"Bohai Chen."

Scott blazed through a red light and floored it onto the freeway. "What makes you think he's our guy, Murph?"

"There's no simple way to answer that because this guy is like a ghost. Many years ago, he held an official title within the Chinese government. Then, nearly twenty years ago, he vanished from public record. No position. No title. And there's no record of his switching back into the private sector. He was just gone. But he's been spotted and photographed a couple times since. He always has tight security, and anyone who gets caught taking a picture of him gets tossed into prison. The cost of living in a country without freedom, right? And one of the organizations he's been spotted dealing with is Lotus Global."

Murph fell quiet, letting his words settle.

It was Jason who eventually broke the silence. "Who do you think he is?"

Murph sighed. "I think he's the head of China's unrestricted warfare program and the guy who planned out the whole attack in Iceland and the scheme to re-release smallpox on the world. I think he's the one who pinned the whole thing on General Kang and the other North Koreans. And I think he's the one who's put a bounty on Jason's head and ignited the ploy to get the US to go to war with Iran."

"You think China's behind all of this?" Alejandra said.

Murph shook his head. "No. Just this guy and his clandestine group acting outside the law. Free rein. Plausible deniability and all that. But I won't say that the Chinese government wouldn't benefit from the US going to war with Iran. It's a gray area."

"It usually is in politics and war," Scott said.

Jason rubbed his chin while watching the city fly by. "Any idea where we can find him?"

Murph smiled. "Well, that's the thing. The data point that really sealed the deal for me was the other info I managed to obtain, along with the IP address. Mainly, the device's location, based on its network. The computer that was hooked up to the live feed of the attack on the container ship was in Macau, in a skyrise office owned by Lotus Global. And one that Bohai Chen has been spotted near before. He was also known for—back in the years he was public—being an avid gambler and boxing enthusiast, making Sin Island a favorite place of his. That place makes Las Vegas look like small potatoes."

"How certain are you it's him?" Scott asked.

"Ninety-eight percent," Murph replied immediately, as if his analytical mind had already performed the rough math. "But even if it somehow isn't him, that server was receiving a signal from this skyscraper in Macau. We know that for certain."

Scott nodded. He slipped out his phone and made a call to their jet's pilot. Both of the team's aircraft were parked at the airport's private terminal, but they'd need the supersonic speed demon if they were going to reach the Chinese island in time.

Jason leaned forward and eyed Scott through the rearview mirror. "You mentioned something about us having a bigger problem?"

Scott floored the gas even more, pushing the vehicle to its limits. "It's the Joint Chiefs. They want an update . . . and it's not looking good."

They reached Cape Town International ten minutes later, Scott flooring the SUV at over a hundred miles per hour for most of the route. They rushed through the security checkpoints, and he drove them right onto the tarmac, racing toward the private jet that was already warming up, alongside a team of workers loading a large crate through its rear door.

Scott braked to a hard stop at the base of the steps, and the five of them jumped out and hustled into the cabin. It looked almost cramped with everyone inside, the sleek aircraft nearing its max occupancy.

The pilots swiftly taxied, and they were in the air five minutes after they'd boarded. The meteor shower had ended, leaving only fixed stars hanging in the darkness overhead.

Jason stepped into the bathroom and looked in the mirror. He was battered and bruised. His face was cut up and beginning to swell at the cheek where the assassin struck him in the castle. He splashed cold water over his face and then changed out of his soaked clothes and into a pair of black tactical pants and a matching T-shirt.

When he returned to the main cabin, the rest of the group was huddled in front of the monitor set against the wall. Murph hooked up his computer as Jason settled in with the others. There was a fresh pot of coffee, and he poured a mug, relishing the hot, caffeinated beverage as Murph booted up a video chat.

A familiar image appeared of the Joint Chiefs in the Situation Room, all twelve of them seated and wearing full dress uniforms. There was enough brass to sink a rowboat—a combined four hundred years of military experience between them. And all eyes were on the team.

President Martin was at his place at the head of the table, flanked by the most powerful military leaders in the country. The president looked tired and upset. "What have you got?" he said, getting straight to it. "Did you capture the criminal hacker? Did you get him to talk?"

Jason said, "Cipher got away, Mr. President."

"But the mission was successful," Scott chimed in.

"So, then, you have proof of who's behind this?"

"Cipher was behind this," Scott said. "Now we're going after the one who hired him."

"Which could be anybody? It could be the Iranian government, right?"

"No, sir. We were able to figure out that the guy who hired Cipher is in Macau, and we're—"

The president waved a hand. "We're out of time."

Jason leaned forward. "With respect, sir, we still have five hours."

"Not anymore. There's been another attack, as I'm sure you've heard on the news by now."

"I watched live footage of it, Mr. President," Jason said, getting everyone in the room's attention. "Cipher played a live feed from a drone near the container ship. I watched it happen because he orchestrated the attack, and he used the other cruise missile he stole from the Iranian arsenal earlier this year."

The cabin and Situation Room both fell silent. The military leaders exchanged glances with each other and the president.

Scott cleared his throat and stepped in. "I don't have to tell any of you this, but there's a fine line here, and once it's crossed, there's no going back. Give us the rest of the time—just five more hours—and we'll get you proof of who's really behind all of this."

President Martin shook his head. "I can't do it, Coop. Do you have any idea what the repercussions will be if we fail to take immediate decisive action and you're wrong?"

"Yes, sir. But we're right. And I'm willing to stake not just my reputation, but the reputation of our entire group on that."

President Martin paused a beat, steepling his fingers. He looked across the table at his advisors, each in turn, then shook his head again. "I can't, Coop. We can't. There's too much at stake here to wait any longer."

"Mr. President," Jason said. "As a covert servant of our nation, as an American, and as a man, I ask you to reconsider."

The president stared at Jason a long moment, then pushed his chair back and stood. Jason's words were reminiscent of something the commander in chief had said during their first time meeting at Capitol Hill Books in DC. President Martin had wanted to thank Jason personally for all he'd done, and he'd told Jason that he owed him one.

The president paced across the room with his hands on his hips. He eyed something on the back wall, then he turned around and gestured to one of the Joint Chiefs.

The screen went black.

"What happened?" Jason said.

Scott waved a hand. "Don't worry. He just wants a moment to talk it over without us."

Given the intensity of the situation, things like formality were cast to the wayside. Getting this done quickly and efficiently was the name of the game.

"What if they go through with their mobilizations?" Jason said.

Scott folded his arms. "Then . . . it won't be good."

"But we know this wasn't the Iranians," Alejandra said. "We know that, right? So why would they do this?"

"There are bigger, more complicated things at play here," Scott said. "The world is watching President Martin and the US government closely right now. And frankly, at face value, his response to recent incidents could be perceived as weak."

"So, it's all about politics?" Alejandra said.

"No. It's about maintaining the strong, formidable, composed, and in control face that is the United States. It's about authority. He's got a dozen military men telling him that right now. And hundreds of analysts and strategists behind the scenes are running the odds and predicting the outcomes. I don't envy his position."

Jason said, "If they make the move . . . If they mobilize, then like you said, things will get ugly, fast. Even if we do figure out who's really responsible, it'll likely be too late. Too much damage will have already been caused."

The screen blinked, and the Joint Chiefs and president appeared again.

President Martin looked composed and decisive. "The decision has been made to green-light military advancement. But we've made adjustments to the operation, primarily to the initial stages. We've switched things around, and the mobilization of any nearby ground forces won't occur until after we've moved the Truman carrier strike group into position in the Gulf of Oman. This is a move that will take some time—just over five hours, based on the strike group's current position."

He paused, observing the reaction of the covert group.

"You will use that time to figure out who this son of a bitch is, or we're going in hot. We'll have no other choice. It's come to that. Understood?"

"Understood, Mr. President," Scott said.

"And one more thing," General Richardson said. "If you're heading to China, you'll be completely on your own. We can't offer support of any kind. Zero backup, either militarily or politically. We won't acknowledge our awareness of your presence there, and we'll deny your affiliation if you get caught."

The five of them exchanged glances, then President Martin looked into the camera. "Godspeed."

FORTY

MACAU, CHINA

THE DISTANCE FROM Cape Town to Macau is just over seven thousand miles, crossing the Indian Ocean and much of Southeast Asia. It was a journey that took at least thirteen hours for a typical commercial airliner, but their jet was on pace to make the leap in just over four hours. It was a good thing, as time wasn't exactly on their side.

They'd get into Macau with less than an hour to not only locate Chen, but to get him to talk, and then hopefully work an extraction plan into the mix for after the fact. None of the team members had to think hard to guess what would happen if anyone got caught.

They were on their own, and the clock was ticking. And three and a half hours into the flight, the bad news continued when the pilots hailed ATCs at Macau International. After a quick exchange, the captain strode back into the cabin to notify the group that due to recent global incidents, all international private flights into the country would be stopped and searched on the tarmac, and all the occupants would undergo a more thorough-than-usual immigration process.

"This whole thing just keeps getting better and better," Scott said.

The pilot stood tall. "We're thirty minutes out. What do you want to do?"

It was a stern question—one that demanded a good, confident answer.

"What about Hong Kong airport?" Jason said.

The pilot shook his head. "Same story there. And the same with Zhuhai and Guangzhou Baiyun."

"And Hong Kong Airport is at least an hour from the heart of Macau anyway," Murph said.

"He's right," Alejandra said. She and Finn studied a GPS image of Macau, the Zhujiang River Estuary, and Hong Kong. "Even with non-existent traffic, we'd never make it in time."

Jason thought hard, then gazed aft. "We should land in Hong Kong. It'll be less suspicious that way . . . in case I get caught."

Scott studied the operative with a narrowed gaze, then he looked toward the storage space at the rear of the aircraft and back to the pilot. "Hong Kong it is, Captain."

The man bowed slightly and headed back into the cockpit.

"You two heard us, right?" Finn looked up from the monitor. "We'll never make it that far."

"We don't need to," Scott said.

"And it doesn't matter because we'll be stuck on the tarmac for close to an hour, easy," Alejandra said. "A Chinese government search at a time like this? It'll take forever, if they even let us into the country."

"They don't need to let *us* in," Scott added. "By that point, Jason will already be on the ground in Macau."

Alejandra shook her head. "How do you figure that?"

The group looked confused, then Jason rose and motioned his head toward the back. "Because I'm getting off early."

There wasn't time to properly vet the plan. No time to test it for holes and implement backups. If troubles arose, Jason would have to rely on instinct to adapt, and they'd be winging much of it. Minor portions of the initial plan could be used, but they'd had no choice but to scrap most of it. Jason would be on his own, and if he couldn't find a way, the whole endeavor would be for nothing.

Passing through the rear door, Jason opened a large storage box and removed a blacked-out parachute and matching helmet. The headgear was specially designed, with altitude, wind speed, and distance-to-target indications on the inside of the smart glass display.

While the team helped Jason prep his gear, Finn and Murph rolled out the latest prototype of the team's extraction drone, the big, powerful unmanned vehicle's three rotors folded into the body for ease of travel. They expanded and performed checks on the device.

The space was cramped, barely tall enough to stand, and just twenty feet long. The aircraft had been designed for speed, not long-haul transport. But she had special features implemented, including an airtight rear door so the interior could be separated and the main cabin could remain pressurized during high-altitude jumps.

Once everything was ready, they ran through the plan once more using three-dimensional images of the city. Jason's target was one of the tallest skyscrapers in the metropolis, located just off the famous Cotai Strip. He'd be aiming for a big garden that jutted out a quarter of the way from the top and was adjacent to the offices of Lotus Global.

Once the loose plan was set, Scott headed to the cockpit to give altitude and approach instructions to the pilots. The jet adjusted its course just slightly to give Jason the optimal jump spot.

"We're five minutes out," Scott said as he returned to the group.

Jason finished tightening his gear and strapping his pistol, spare magazine, knife, and other gadgets into place. He also positioned a pair of night vision binoculars over his helmet, then Finn attached a bodycam to his lightweight bulletproof vest, the device so small and discreet it was nearly imperceptible.

They could feel the plane descending, and the pilot's voice sounded through a nearby speaker, letting them know they were two minutes out.

Now at just six thousand feet, they stepped to the rear and opened the loading door. A flat expanse of the dark South China Sea came into view.

The wind howled past Jason as he stepped to the edge, grabbed hold of the overhead, and looked out just as city lights came into view. Their approach lined up well, the jet soaring over the gambling mecca before reaching the airport in Hong Kong. Jason preferred to make the jump at a more typical height of around fifteen thousand feet, but the close proximity of the Hong Kong Airport required the pilots to descend significantly as not to look suspicious to ATCs.

Scott shouted over the wail of the engines. "No one better for the job, Jase."

Jason gave his team a thumbs-up, then stepped toward the door and jumped out without a moment's hesitation.

During his first stint at Tenth Circle, Jason had been sent to the Army's Jump School in Fort Benning, Georgia, where he'd been trained by the military's elite skydivers and completed over a hundred jumps. The familiar free-falling sensation took over—a hyper-awareness of the loud noise and the vast sky—the rush of adrenaline and the feeling of his stomach shooting up toward his head as he swiftly accelerated, hitting terminal velocity in twelve seconds.

The sounds of the plane died away at his back as he soared toward the tightly packed, colorful high-rises below. Las Vegas is America's playground, but Jason was free-falling toward the World's playground. He could feel the electricity—the thump of the thick concentration of life and colors and sounds beneath him. Lines of vehicles weaved through the metal, neon jungle, and hundreds of thousands of people walked the dense city streets.

The tops of the buildings drew near, the city growing bigger at a seemingly faster click. Jason stared at his target—the dark skyscraper right in front of him. The screen of his helmet locked onto his destination and gave him precise measurements, allowing him to tweak his free-fall position as necessary. The low-altitude jump didn't last long.

Just thirty-two seconds after tossing himself out of the back of the aircraft, he'd already plummeted four thousand five hundred feet. He pulled the ripcord, and the chute burst free, straightening and catching the air. It jerked Jason back, and everything went calm and still in an instant.

Just over a thousand feet above the earth, he held tight to the risers and steered as he soared under the tops of the tallest buildings. The sounds of the city grew louder, a constant, chaotic symphony of chatter and music and engines and horns. The heartbeat of a money-pumped destination that had recently exploded onto the global scene.

Jason homed in on the waypoint while hanging under the canopy. He slid up the visor of his helmet, then positioned the night vision goggles over his eyes and scanned his approaching landing zone less than a hundred feet away and half that distance below.

The garden veranda was roughly the size of a basketball court, with a fountain in the middle and pathways and hedges and trees along the sides. A massive door was open, revealing a well-lit meeting area flanked by office spaces.

"Garden's clear," Jason said, triggering his internal mic.

He aimed for the far corner of the garden, where a long stretch of grass was shielded by a towering ginkgo tree.

Jason's boots struck the grass at a run, and he pivoted and dropped to a knee. He popped the left riser strap of his chute so a rogue evening gust didn't drag him over the side of the building. Then he swiftly collapsed the canopy, unfastened the straps, balled up the chute, and crammed everything into a dump pouch. He unclipped the pouch and stashed it between a ring of tall flowers and the base of the tree.

"On the ground and moving in," he said before removing and powering off the helmet.

He left his helmet in the shadows with his chute and harness, then pulled out a ski mask and slid it snug over his head. Once ready, he crept along the hedge for a view of the entrance into the office space. Everything was immaculate. The grass was perfectly cut, the bushes trimmed smooth, and the walkways set in carefully cut and placed slabs of granite. There was a hint of jasmine in the air, mixing with the ocean and smog and wafting aromas from a thousand high-end restaurants below.

He took post opposite the entrance and peeked over the hedge. The interior was spotless. Jason had been raised in a world of luxury, so he knew expensive and high-end when he saw it: glossy marble floors, elegant artwork on the walls, and a long glass table and leather office chairs.

The huge door opened up to a central meeting space, then branched off to individual offices. A floor up and to his left, situated in the corner, looked like a private office with its own veranda offering sweeping views of both the city and waterfront. Through one of the windows, he saw a man seated at a desk. Though Jason only had a side profile and the man was far off, he saw faint resemblances to the image Murph had shown him of Lotus Global's young CEO. He marked the office as his destination.

Just as Jason was about to step out from the shadows, movement appeared. Two formally dressed night security guards marched out from the central area and into the garden. They stood at the edge of the bleeding light, then spread apart and stood like statues with their hands at their sides.

Jason examined their positions relative to him and the door. Given their distance from each other, engaging them would be tough and nearly impossible to do by himself without alerting others inside.

He checked his watch. They had thirty-seven minutes.

The two guards moved in unison, turning away from each other and striding along the opposite straightaway of the rectangular path with their flashlights on.

Jason tracked them both. The guy to the left was closer and would cut around to reach his position in under a minute. But the other guy was heading toward his stashed chute on the opposite side. He doubted a normal security guard would spot it, but the two men closing in on him didn't seem normal. They looked and moved like experienced operatives.

Jason made a split-second decision and cut left. Without a sound, he reached the end of the path and crouched at the corner of the hedge as the nearest guard approached. He squatted lower and grabbed his knife while remaining steady and calm, knowing he'd have one chance to take the guy down silently.

A step before the guard reached the corner, Jason burst around and drove forward and up, catching the guard in a rapid motion with his arm clamped around his mouth. The guy had a brief moment to squirm and reach for his weapon before Jason subdued him and forced him into the shadows at the base of the hedge.

Ten seconds later, the guy was limp. Jason re-sheathed his knife and grabbed the flashlight. He poked his head around the corner just as the other guy reached the long straightaway, but Jason couldn't make out anything from that far. The light was blinding, and he couldn't see anything other than a dark outline of the guy's features. It gave Jason an idea.

He rose, held the light directly in front of him, and shined the beam ahead while retrieving his suppressed pistol. He stepped around the corner, shining the bright wave right at the guard.

They moved toward each other, Jason trying his best to act natural as they closed in. Fifty feet. Then thirty. Then Twenty.

The guy paused and held up a hand. "Would you shine that somewhere else?" he said in Mandarin.

Jason tilted the beam away, and the guard blinked, then his mouth dropped as he stared at the barrel of Jason's Walther aiming straight at him. The guard lurched back and reached for his weapon. Jason pulled the trigger, firing a suppressed .22-caliber round into the guy's left thigh. He fell hard, his upper body striking the ground.

Jason raced forward and silenced him with a kick across his forehead. With both guards down, he dropped the flashlight, then turned to face the door. Holding his weapon with two hands, he cut across the garden, walking through the middle breaks in the hedges.

The vast meeting area was empty. He moved inside, cutting between two ivory pool tables. He veered left, wanting to reach the upstairs corner office before anyone realized he was there.

Finn's voice crackled through his earpiece. "The drone's airborne, Jase. Had to take off in secret while taxiing, but it's heading across the river and toward the tower now."

"Copy that, Finn."

He entered an adjoining space with two empty secretary desks facing each other. Ahead was a glass staircase that wrapped around to the next level, and as Jason approached it, he heard footsteps coming from an opposite entryway. He turned rapidly, bolted for cover along the wall, and remained crouched until a guard walked into view. He sprang up and chopped a hand into the guy's throat. As the man gagged and his head snapped forward, Jason hooked an arm around his back and forced his forehead into the corner of the nearest desk. The moment the bone struck the hardwood, the man went lifeless, curled up at Jason's feet.

Jason waited, listening carefully, and covering both entry points with his pistol. When no one appeared, he resumed his charge toward the stairs, taking them on two at a time with his weapon raised and ready. At the top, he came to another grand desk and a pair of double doors. He calmed his breath, then grabbed the handle and jerked it open. Flooding inside, he took aim across the oversized office.

Two leather couches faced each other near a waxed bubinga desk. A lavishly dressed Chinese man sat under the glow of a lamp, typing away at his computer. The guy froze when Jason entered, aghast as he noticed the sudden intruder.

"Who the hell are you?" he said in Mandarin as he slowly rose to his feet and reached for something under his desk.

"Hands in the air," Jason hissed, pointing the pistol at the guy as he pushed across the room, the door swinging shut at his back.

The man looked spooked, but he kept his hands down, still reaching for something out of sight. Jason pulled the trigger, blasting a round through the guy's right shoulder. The force of the impact spun him out of his chair, and he cried out wildly as he slammed backward and flailed onto the marble floor near the window.

Jason closed the distance, standing over him with his sights leveled on his forehead. The businessman cried and cursed, and he pressed a hand to the wound as blood flowed out between his fingers.

"Shut up, or I'll fire another one." Jason grabbed the guy's collar of his silk dress shirt and held him up to the light to get a good look at his face. The man was wincing and shaking, the skin around his eyes scrunched up from the extreme pain. Jason recognized him from the photograph. It was Ru Xiang, the CEO of Lotus Global.

"What the hell do you want?"

"I want you to tell me about Iran. I want you to tell me who ordered the attack in Texas and Florida and Hormuz."

The man's eyes widened, and he shook his head. "I have no idea what you're talking about. You've got the wrong person. I—"

Jason whacked him across the face. "Bullshit!"

As the businessman fell to the floor again, Jason removed a hacking device from his pocket and plugged it into Xiang's computer.

"Let me know when you're in," he said into his earpiece.

Two seconds later, Murph said, "Got it. And he's already logged in, so dealing with the security won't be as bad."

Jason turned his attention back to the man at his feet. The blood was pooling and staining his expensive clothes. He figured he had about two minutes before the guy lost too much blood and passed out.

"You keep playing dumb, and you're gonna be dead. You understand?" He grabbed the guy's shirt again and muscled his head off the floor. "Now, tell me where Bohai Chen is."

The guy's tear-filled eyes widened again at the mention of the name. His mouth opened, and he shook his head back and forth. "I do business with Mr. Chen, but I have no idea what you're talking about."

"We traced a connection between the attacks in Hormuz to this office, Xiang."

"I don't know where Mr. Chen is. But I'm sure he can clear this up."

"He was here earlier tonight, right?"

"I . . . I believe so. I don't know. Damn, this hurts." He cried again and rolled side to side.

Jason knew the pain the guy was feeling. He'd been shot before and was familiar with the extreme nature of it. But this was an office worker who probably squealed when he got a paper cut. This was a guy not used to such extreme pain.

Murph's voice returned in his ear. "I've gone through his files. This is a dead end, Jase. The computer's hard drive is mostly empty. There's barely anything here, let alone anything that points to a link with Cipher or the attacks."

Jason turned his head in frustration. A glance at his watch told him they had just twenty minutes left. Tightening his grip on the CEO, Jason forced the shaky man's head off the floor once again. "Yes or no, Xiang. Was Chen here?"

Xiang paused, then closed his eyes and nodded vigorously.

"Where is he? Tell me, and I might not shoot you again. *Don't* tell me, and I'm going to empty this clip into your extremities, and you're going to bleed to death right here on your office floor."

Xiang sobbed. "I don't know where he is."

"Where is he?" Jason shouted, shoving the barrel of his pistol into the man's gut.

"I don't know!"

Jason jolted and turned as the massive office doors slammed open. He shifted his aim, pointing his pistol toward the entryway, then felt his stomach drop as half a dozen guards shouldering assault rifles stormed inside, every barrel aimed straight at him.

FORTY-ONE

THE SIX MEN stood evenly spaced with their rifles raised like a firing squad. Jason couldn't engage them—not on his own and just thirty feet away. By the time he raised his weapon and got a shot off, he'd be riddled with lead.

Jason slowly reached his hands for the vaulted ceiling while Xiang cowered and cried at his feet.

"Release the magazine," one of the men barked.

Jason flicked the release button with his thumb, and the metal clip slid free, rattling to the floor.

"Aim the weapon toward you," the man said, "and set it on the desk."

Jason did as he said, rotating the weapon so he could grip it backward, then slowly planted it on the hardwood.

Half of the group closed in while the other three hung back and fanned out to provide cover. Two went for Jason, ordering him to lay flat on the floor before shoving a knee into his back and patting him down. They removed his earpiece, knife, and spare magazine. The third guy went for Xiang, heaving the squealing businessman off the floor and practically carrying him for the door.

Keeping Jason pinned, the men reached for the thick Velcro straps securing his vest in place. They tore the left one free with a loud rip, then a new voice filled the air.

"Get him up."

Displaying complete obedience, the two men stopped what they were doing and muscled Jason to his feet. They ushered him around the desk, and Jason got his first look at the man who'd spoken.

He appeared behind the three still aiming at him, sauntering into the glow of the desk lamp. He placed a hand on Xiang as the bleeding man was led out, then he turned forward.

As the man moved closer, the lighting offered Jason a good look at his face for the first time. It was Bohai Chen. Jason was sure of it. The middle-aged man before him perfectly matched the pictures he'd seen.

"Nothing tests a man's loyalty like a real trial by fire," Chen said, shooting a glance back at Xiang. "Do you know why he lied so convincingly? Because he's been properly trained and conditioned. And he's witnessed what happens to those who betray me."

The two men stopped Jason in front of the desk, both gripping tight to an arm.

Chen moved toward Jason, then grabbed a chair and spun it around. With a flick of his hand, Jason was forced into it.

Three more guards stomped into the room.

"We've completed the sweep," one of them said to Chen. "The offices and balcony are clear. We found his parachute in the garden. He's alone."

"A lone operative?" Chen said. "I'm insulted." He ordered the three men to stay by the doors, then stepped closer to Jason and planted his hands on his hips. "Did you really think we wouldn't be expecting you, Jason Wake?"

He grabbed the top of Jason's ski mask and pulled the fabric off his face. Jason remained focused and unfazed, staring back into Chen's eyes.

The man tossed the ski mask aside and stood tall with his hands clasped behind his back. "Though I must say, I didn't expect you to arrive so soon. You are indeed a man of incredible means and drive. Much like myself. I respect your passion and grit, but you just pushed too far and too long. You've been a pest that just won't be squashed. And you've really pissed me off."

"All I've done is—"

Jason was silenced by a sudden, powerful smack across the back of his head. He twisted and clenched his jaw, fighting to brush off the blow like it was nothing.

Jason sat up straight, and Chen held up a hand. "Let's hear the man speak."

Jason took a few slow breaths, then narrowed his gaze at Chen. "All I've done is try to prevent a war. Pissing you off was just a bonus."

The powerful man smiled. "War is inevitable. To think otherwise is to have a severely misguided understanding of human nature. But the nature of war, the details, the key players, and the time and place of the major conflicts . . . those can all be orchestrated. Planned out ahead of time for the eventual good of your nation. It's called taking the initiative."

"That's what you call it? Framing another country by launching stolen missiles at civilians?"

The man smiled broader, then paced slowly back and forth, like a renowned professor giving a lecture. "The world is changing at a rapid pace. And with it, the nature of global warfare. It will be the nation that adapts best to harnessing unconventional tactics that will come out on top. Myself, and the program I've created, are the visionary tips of the spear in this new way of doing things."

"Your English needs some work. Visionary? I believe you meant *deranged*."

Chen chuckled. "Your naivety is perfectly symbolic of what will bring about your nation's downfall."

"And your pessimistic view of mankind's future will lead to nothing but mutual destruction in the end. You're right. The world is changing rapidly. And mankind will either band together, or all of us will die."

"Band together? You are a fascinating enigma, Jason Wake. Effective, no doubt about that, but fatally optimistic. You may have gotten lucky preventing the release of the virus, but this entire plan is already in motion. War between the US and Iran is now inevitable. Our work has assured it."

"The only thing that's inevitable is your impending death. You'll pay for everything you've done, including the Texas attack." Jason began to shake, the rage inside him boiling over. He gazed ferociously at Chen, his muscles flexing, his breathing quickening.

"That little attack was written off as a failure. But then I found out about your notorious hero, retired Brigadier General Marcus Chapman, and I felt better about the operation. A consolatory prize." He shrugged. "And we got you in the end anyway."

Jason's eyes remained locked on the man as he continued.

"You know, I was going to end it quickly, Wake. I was going to give you the honor of a bullet to the head. But now, like I said, you've really pissed me off. You see, we know you're not supposed to be here. That this whole thing will have no official support from your government. That no one will come for you. Instead of a quick death, you will be tortured, Wake. Again and again. And you will suffer malnourishment that will take you right to the brink of death, but we won't grant you that mercy. Then, once I'm finished with you, you will spend the rest of your life in a prison camp, forced to do manual labor until your body breaks apart and you slowly fade away into oblivion."

Chen gave Jason a final smug, satisfied look, then signaled to the guards at his sides. They tugged Jason by the arms and lifted him out of the chair. Two of the other guards rolled in a cart with a black body bag resting on top of it. They wheeled it up to Jason, then one of them removed a syringe from a plastic case. He gave the plunger a soft push to make sure the fluid was flowing through, then turned to Jason.

"Don't worry, Wake," Chen said. "You won't feel a thing, for now. When you wake up, however, that will be a different story."

Jason was held tight as the guard stepped closer with the syringe. He struggled to break free, but the men were strong. Chen seemed to enjoy it as the guy chose a spot on Jason's right shoulder, then hovered the needle over his target. He was just about to stab when a flash of light shined into the room from the window at their backs. The brilliant beam flashed into Chen's and his men's eyes and rapidly swept across the room.

The three guards providing cover shifted their aim and opened fire, blasting rounds through the glass.

Everything slowed as Jason's mind worked in overdrive, a flood of adrenaline and training taking over. He needed to move. He needed to do something. This was it. Now or never.

Raising his right leg, he jammed his heel into the instep of the guard to his right. The guy loosened his grip, and Jason tore his arm free and threw his right fist across his body, twisting and bashing his knuckles into the throat of the guard to his left. Then Jason yanked the other arm free in a flash and came back with his right elbow, smashing the bone into the first guy's forehead.

It happened in a blink—a rapid display of efficient, deadly muscle memory. The sounds of the gunfire and crashing glass, and the confusion from the mysterious flash of light, gave him just the distraction he needed.

Jason launched forward just as Chen processed what was happening. Wrapping an arm around the man, Jason swiftly changed directions and threw himself backward, carrying the criminal with him as he flew past the chair and onto the desk. He held tight to the man as they rolled over the smooth hardwood, whirling off the edge and onto the floor on the other side. Jason forced the man into submission, his right arm around the guy's throat and the other flexed across his chest.

Jason rose to his feet.

As straggling shards of glass rained down at their back, the guards ceased firing, all of them taking aim at Jason.

Chen said, "What now, Jason Wake? This building is swarming with my men. There's no way out of this for you."

Using the man as a human shield, Jason heaved a step backward, his boots crackling on the carpet of loose glass. The guards followed suit, moving closer and branching out for better angles.

Jason forced his way back another step, then another, then manhandled Chen out onto the balcony.

Chen chuckled. "There's nowhere to run, Wake."

Jason pushed back another step. The wind was powerful, and the sounds of the lively city were loud.

"There's one way," Jason whispered, keeping the man in front of him.

Chen looked left and right, then turned frantic. "You're crazy."

"If I go down, I'm taking you with me."

Jason forced them back yet another half step. Chen fought to break free, but Jason hooked his arm around him and leapt, keeping a firm grasp around his neck. In a flash of unexpected movement, they both flew over the railing, spinning out over six hundred feet of open air.

FORTY-TWO

THE TWO MEN plummeted headlong into a tumultuous free fall, quickly picking up speed. Chen yelled maniacally, cursing Jason as they spun. Jason maintained his grip, holding tight to the criminal leader as the floors of the building blurred past them and the mass of lights and streets and people below came into focus.

They fell into the void for five maddening seconds before the sounds of buzzing rotors resounded below them, and their bodies struck a weave of cross-connecting fibers. They jolted, the landing knocking the air from their lungs even as the net lowered rapidly, giving in with their force. The sounds of the rotors intensified to a screeching whine as they continued to descend for two seconds before leveling off and angling into a horizontal path, soaring along the side of the building less than fifty feet above the ground.

Jason maintained his firm grip on Chen, but angled his head back and looked up at the drone, the powerful unmanned aircraft blasting them back up and through the heart of the city. They promptly accelerated to a hundred and fifty miles per hour, weaving in and out of buildings and casinos. Breaking out of the city, they blasted over the waterfront, then the world below flattened and turned pitch black as they roared out over the South China Sea.

The aircraft descended, flying a hundred feet over the water and then accelerated even more, reaching its loaded-down top speed of a blistering two hundred miles per hour. The dark world rushed past, the slightly white-capped sea reeling in beneath them.

Jason adjusted his grip on Chen, then realized the guy was unconscious, the shock of the fall and sudden catch apparently having knocked him out. He peered ahead at the seemingly endless horizon. Turning back, he watched as the blazing city grew smaller to the north, then eventually vanished.

He wondered what the plan was from there—where he'd rendezvous with the others. But the little vehicle just kept cruising along, zipping across the sky like it was possessed.

Jason checked his watch. The timer indicated exactly two minutes left in the countdown. With no way to communicate with the other members of the squad, he could only watch, shielding the wind from his eyes as the seconds counted down and then reached zero.

He looked down and closed his eyes, hoping for the best but expecting the worst. The drone continued on, soaring for just over twenty minutes, then it finally slowed. Jason ran through the quick math in his head and figured they'd traveled around seventy miles since leaving Macau.

The extraction drone slowed to a hover, then descended and remained suspended over thirty feet of water. Jason looked around. The only thing in sight for miles was the occasional distant fishing boat.

He lay there another minute, then large bubbles surfaced in the dark, ominous stretch of water, as if an unknown beast was about to emerge. Then a tall, tower-like structure broke through the water. It was the sail of a submarine. The structure rose, then the rest of the boat started appearing, the topside hull barely splashing through. Jason recognized it as a Virginia-class submarine, the newest class of the United States Navy's fast attack fleet.

A man in dark coveralls and a harness poked out of the top, followed right after by another, and they waved the craft over. The drone angled and flew over the conning tower, descending slowly and allowing Jason to climb out of the net and onto the deck. They dragged Chen off, easing him onto the deck beside them.

One of the men was nearly Jason's size but about twenty years older and wore the collar device of a commander.

"Jason Wake," he said, stretching out a hand. "I'm Commander Harris, commanding officer of the USS *Hawaii*. Welcome aboard."

The drone landed on the hull, and Jason, along with the help of two sailors, climbed down and quickly collapsed the device so it could fit inside. The crew looped a line around Chen's shoulders to lower him down through the hatch, then Jason and the others lowered the drone and climbed down.

Chen was tied up and taken to the lower level, and the commander led Jason into the control room. Seconds after the hatch was secured, the order was given for the boat to dive, and less than five minutes after it had surfaced, the *Hawaii* submerged back into the South China Sea.

"Thanks for the lift, sir," Jason said.

He admired the members of America's silent service as they manned their stations. They were some of the best and most highly trained sailors in the fleet.

Jason was about to admit he thought he was a goner, when the commander stepped forward and cut him off. "I've been ordered to learn as little as possible regarding your mission."

Seeing everything was taken care of with the dive and that they were on their ordered course, the commander ushered Jason into the wardroom. He gestured for two young officers to clear out, then he shut the door behind them.

"I've been in contact with Mr. Cooper," Commander Harris said. "That's how we were relayed your position." He cracked open a laptop, then established comms with Scott. "Let me know if you need anything, Mr. Wake." The captain stepped out and shut the door behind him.

Scott spoke through a wave of static. "You reading me, Jase?"

The crackling sounds receded, and Jason replied, "Loud and clear, Scottie. Tell Finn nice catch."

Scott chuckled. "He'll never let you forget that one."

"I hope not. That was a move for the ages. You guys get the footage?"

"Just got done showing it to the president and Joint Chiefs. They've put a red light on further mobilization and are working harder to conduct talks with Iranian representatives. Well done getting Chen to admit to everything."

Jason thought back to the interaction in the highrise office and how his bodycam had recorded the entire thing, transmitting the footage to Scott and the rest of the team. The man had brought his own downfall, confessing to all of the attacks they'd pinned on the Islamic Republic of Iran.

"It's over, kid," Scott said. "And with Chen in custody, who knows what else we can extract."

Jason relaxed on the bench seat, his head leaning back against the paneling. He looked around the wardroom. "I thought President Martin said we'd be completely on our own. How'd you get him to agree to pick us up?"

"Fortunately, the *Hawaii* had been steaming relatively nearby on its way back to Guam. And I may have placed a call to the vice admiral of the Navy to help plead our case for the military to aid with extraction. The drone's equipped with radar avoidance technology, and the *Hawaii* was far enough out to sea for the unplanned brief surfacing to go unnoticed. As far as the Chinese government is concerned, you were never there."

Jason smiled for what felt like the first time in forever. "You guys back in the air?"

"Taxiing now. There'll be a Jayhawk inbound to rendezvous and pick you and Chen up once you're farther off the coast. I'll keep you updated, and we'll see you back Stateside."

They ended the call, and Jason sat listening to the hum of machinery and the hushed chatter coming from the nearby galley. His adrenaline was wearing off, and fatigue was beginning to set in.

He couldn't believe he'd made it out alive. He thought for sure he'd die back in the building or be taken prisoner. He'd accepted it, and the sacrifice would've been worth it. Getting Chen to admit to all he'd done in order to fulfill their mission and prevent a war was more important than his life.

But he *did* make it out. His team pulled through, and somehow, he snuck free with his life. Now there he was, sitting in the wardroom of an advanced warship, hundreds of feet underwater.

He scanned the room, then closed his eyes, feeling a wave of relief, like an enormous weight had lifted off his shoulders.

FORTY-THREE

**SIX DAYS LATER
BROOKLYN, NY**

A CROWD OF OVER two hundred people surrounded the casket, their breath steaming in the winter air. The sky was big and clear, the sun shining through breaks in the towering leafless trees.

Jason stood in the back near the base of a maple tree, his hands clasped in front of him and his head slightly bowed. Behind him, up the well-manicured green slope of Cypress Hills National Cemetery, were lines of white headstones marking the final resting places of some of America's greatest citizens—veterans who'd fought bravely, along with some of their immediate family members.

Jason's eyes traveled from the casket draped with a crisp American flag, to a picture of Marcus Chapman resting on a stand beside it. His old mentor was wearing his full dress uniform, decorated with medals and ribbons from a lifetime of service to his country. Though his family had been given the opportunity to lay the decorated war hero to rest in Arlington National Cemetery, Marcus had put in his will that he wanted to be buried in the same cemetery as his parents in his home state of New York.

Many of those gathered to pay their respects were uniformed service members. Closest to the reverend was Marcus's family, dozens of his relatives, and his wife and children at the forefront. Some of the highest-ranking military leaders were in attendance, including an unexpected visit from the commander in chief, President Martin himself.

Marcus had been given the highest burial honors, including a twenty-one gun salute. Seven soldiers stood in a neat line with rifles at the ready, and when given the signal, they blasted three volleys into the air, the cracks of gunpowder echoing across the hills.

When the service finished, Marcus's widow, Jayla, led the way, the crowd parting as she and the family walked slowly down a path toward the parking lot. Jason had hoped to steal a word with her at some point to express not only his condolences, but how much Marcus had meant to him. But he'd have to do it another time.

"Glad you made it," a familiar voice said.

Jason turned as Scott Cooper approached him alongside Logan Dodge. Also a veteran of naval special forces, Logan lived down in Key West, and Jason had met him a couple times before—most notably when they'd all teamed up to take down a murdering white supremacist who'd been holding up on the outskirts of the Everglades.

"Good to see you again, Jason," Logan said, extending a hand.

He was nearly as tall as Jason, but leaner and tanner. Clean cut, he had the familiar and untypical air of profound confidence that Scott possessed.

"Scott told me how it happened," Logan continued. "I was sorry to hear of his passing. Marcus was a great man."

"You went to Tenth Circle?" Jason asked.

Logan shook his head. "I was lucky to have had Chappy teach my close-quarters defense class years ago, back when I was a cocky teenager going through the SEAL pipeline. I've lost count of how many times his lessons and maneuvers have saved my life. And I'm sure there are hundreds of operators who'd say the same thing."

Peeling away from a large group, President Martin approached them, surrounded by members of his

Secret Service detail. The bodyguards spread out, giving the group some space as the president greeted Jason.

"It seems like I never get a chance to thank you unless I come to you," the president said while shaking the covert operator's hand. "So, thank you for helping us out of that hot water. And I wanted to let you know I still owe you that favor."

Jason accepted the thanks with a nod but said nothing. He was still too lost in his thoughts. It was hard for him to feel any semblance of good regarding the outcome, when his mentor and friend was resting in a wooden box in the ground fifty yards away.

Scott cleared his throat. "Mr. President, this is Logan Dodge. We served together in the Navy."

"It's a pleasure to meet you, Logan. And your name does sound familiar."

"The honor's mine, sir."

The president eyed him up and down. "Logan, you look like you get a lot of sun. What line of work are you in now?"

"He's not in a line of work," Scott said. "As hard as I tried to get him to join our group . . . He's retired and lives in Key West."

"More like semi-retired," Logan said.

The president smiled. "My dream retirement spot. If all goes well. I keep meaning to plan a visit there."

Logan said, "You'd receive a warm welcome in the Conch Republic, Mr. President. From what I hear, it's been a while since a sitting POTUS has visited the Little White House."

"I might have to take you up on that offer someday."

One of the president's aides approached and whispered in his ear.

President Martin nodded, then said, "Please excuse me. It was a pleasure meeting you."

He gave a final knowing look to Jason, then patted the operative on the back before being swallowed up by a group migrating toward the nearby lot.

"How are things with Chen?" Jason said when it was just the three of them.

Scott shrugged. "About as expected."

Jason clenched his jaw, then looked off into the distance. The shady Chinese man still hadn't said a word since being taken into custody, but that didn't matter. He'd already said enough back in Macau, and the admissions had resulted in loosened tensions between the US and Iran. By then, both sides had withdrawn their mobilized military units, and peace talks resumed. As for China, their government denied any knowledge of a restricted warfare program or Chen's activities—as was also expected.

"The world leaders are on relatively good terms again," Scott said. "That's the most important thing."

Jason fell silent at that. The mission had been a success, but a far from perfect one. Despite their efforts back at the castle in South Africa, and despite Agent Royal's continued hunt, Cipher had slipped through their fingers and escaped. He was still out there, and the powerful mastermind hacker was ever present in Jason's mind.

Wanting some time alone, Jason agreed to meet up with Scott and Logan for dinner later, and the two left him there at the base of the tree. Letting out a long breath, Jason stepped out into the sun's rays and approached the grave with solemn steps. With everyone else having left, he stared down at the casket.

He thought back to the first time he'd met the former Green Beret and flashed through various moments together throughout his training. Then he thought of that last morning and their run, and the thing he'd nearly said but hadn't quite gotten the words out.

Jason breathed in the fresh cool air. "You're a good man, Marcus."

He stood there another minute before hearing the sound of light footsteps at his back. Jayla Chapman used a handkerchief to combat the tears streaking across her cheeks, but it was a losing battle, and they continued to well up as she walked slowly up to the grave. Without a word, she stopped beside Jason.

Feeling the emotional weight of the moment, Jason buckled, dropping to a knee beside her, his head bowed.

She placed a light hand on the top of his head. "He wasn't supposed to talk about his trainees," she said between sniffles, her voice soft and calming. "But he talked about you."

Jason said nothing. He just closed his eyes.

"I hear you were with him when he died. And I want you to know you should feel anything but guilt." She swallowed. "Marcus loved you like a son. He saw great things in you, Jason. And he's watching, you hear me? He's watching, so you need to continue to fight—to charge on, even into assured defeat. To charge on . . ." Then she said the words that struck him right in the heart. "This wasn't your fault, Jason. This wasn't your fault."

Jason composed himself as best as he could, wiping away his own tears, then he looked up at her.

"I'm not sure if you knew," he said, "but there's this remote overlook in Texas that Marcus named after you. We went on a run just before he died, and we watched the sunrise there—the burning fire on the horizon, piercing red, blazing bright on the desert and setting fire to the sky. Marcus said there was only one name fitting for something so beautiful."

She smiled and helped him stand, then they scooped up handfuls of dirt and said goodbye.

— — —

Sometimes, things don't go according to plan. Backup plans fail. Your enemy surprises you, and your entire scheme crumbles to pieces. Sometimes you're forced to run and bide time.

Cipher was no stranger to that method. He'd been on the run for years. It was his way of life, and for much of that life, he'd been a ghost and operating under the strong belief that humanity was chaos. That life was a muddle of madness, and he'd made it his mission to make things as they should be—to throw mankind into its normal, anarchical way of doing things.

But now, again, things had changed. His mission now revolved around one man. And he'd lurk in the shadows and bide his time, as he always did. He'd wait there, watching and listening and preparing. And one day, when his enemies least expected it, he'd strike with a rapid vengeance unlike anything he'd ever dished out before.

His enemies would pay.

Cipher raised his head and slid back his hood, revealing his dark hair and pale features. Staring into a mirror, his lips formed a rancorous smile. Using a black marker, he wrote nine letters onto the dirty mirror: Jason Wake.

Then he stared at the name a moment before crossing it out.

EPILOGUE

TWO WEEKS AFTER the funeral, Jason was back aboard the *Valiant*, steaming across the Caribbean, when he received a call that caused his heart to skip a beat.

Unable to believe what he was hearing, Jason flew north as quickly as possible, and was soon landing in Washington, DC. He rushed across the city, through the doors of George Washington University Hospital, and down the halls to a room in the ICU. His breath escaped his lungs as he stepped inside, the woman lying on the hospital bed and turning her head so their eyes could meet.

Jason swept across the room in a trance and collapsed, throwing his arms around Charlotte Murchison and holding her tight.

It'd been nearly four months since she'd saved his life, then fallen off a rooftop and onto a balcony at the Watergate Hotel. The blow had put her in a coma, and Jason could hardly believe she was awake and hugging him back. It felt more like a dream than reality.

Her father, Frank, who Jason hadn't even noticed, placed a hand on both of them, then stepped out to give them a moment. After holding onto each other, they loosened their grips, and he gazed into her green eyes. Her short dark hair was back, and her face was as beautiful as ever. Her skin was pale but smooth as silk. And Jason couldn't look away from her.

"I'm sorry," he said. "For everything. And I should've been here when you woke up."

"Shh," she said softly, placing a finger to his lips. Charlotte slid her hand behind his head, weaving her fingers through his hair, and pulled him in close enough for their lips to touch.

The feeling was electric and passionate, and neither wanted it to end.

Eventually, she pulled away and smiled. "You were here for me, Jason. You are here."

He stared at her, lost in her eyes. "Is there anything you need? Anything I can get for you?"

She looked away with a mischievous grin. "Well, there is one thing . . . I'm supposed to stick around here for a while. Take it easy and rest and rehab and whatnot. But I've been given a second chance at life, Jason. And from what I hear, I've spent the past four months sleeping in a hospital bed." She wrapped an arm around him, bringing him close again, then whispered into his ear. "Sweep me away, Jason Wake. Sweep me away to someplace warm."

— — —

The amphibious aircraft splashed down into turquoise waters. Easing back on the throttles, Jason motored up to a wooden dock extending out from a picturesque tropical island. After tying off, he helped Charlotte from the plane and then swooped her off her feet and carried her down the planks toward the shore. The beach before them was perfect—a welcoming, crescent-shaped shoreline, with palm trees and rocks at its flanks, and a friendly surf lapping rhythmically against it.

Jason carried her across the beach toward a vast, single-story mansion set on a dramatic outcropping. They climbed a wide set of stone steps up to a sweeping patio that rimmed the beach, then under a shaded area to a massive door that led inside.

The interior of the mansion was unlike anything Charlotte had ever seen, immaculate and lavishly decorated, from hand-carved lignum vitae furniture to

Persian rugs and cashmere blankets. The space was bright and airy, and the entire back wall of the living room was a sliding glass door that revealed an even more impressive backside of the island. A horseshoe-shaped patio with a beautiful swimming pool bordered a curve of low cliffs and a deep lagoon.

Charlotte stared in awe at the incredible abode that was nothing short of a masterful work of art. "This place is amazing."

Jason smiled. "It's called Xanadu Cay for a good reason. And like the exotic utopia from Coleridge's poem, it gets even better the more you look around. I promise."

"You rented this whole place for us?"

"Not exactly. My dad bought this land when I was young and had this place built. I've been coming here since I was a kid. I sold many other properties he left me, but I couldn't bring myself to part with this one."

Her mouth dropped open. "You own this island?"

He clasped her hand. "Come on. Let me give you the full tour."

Xanadu Cay was just over fifteen acres of prime tropical real estate located in remote waters of the Turks and Caicos.

As Jason showed her around, he pointed toward the enclosed lagoon. "The water only gets in and out through underwater caves. Or the occasional swell during a storm."

The feature and the design of the house and outdoor areas around it made it possible for you to enjoy the ocean by beach, or by jumping in from cliffs. And the waters surrounding the exotic palace were sprawling with all sorts of sea life. Jason had a team of caretakers from a nearby island who looked after the place, restocked the fridge and pantry, and would make their meals as desired. With the idyllic atmosphere, Charlotte knew there was no better place in the world for her to rehab her mind and body.

In the mornings, they snorkeled around the island, exploring nooks and crannies and savoring the beautiful scenery. In the afternoons, they lounged under fans and drank smoothies and ate freshly grilled fish. And at night, they got lost in each other, tangling up in the sheets and falling asleep to the sounds of the waves and ocean breeze.

One morning, Jason was lounging on a padded beach chair when he received a text message.

> *Enjoy your paradise while you can, Wake. One day, when you least expect it, we'll meet again. -C*

Jason read the message twice, then looked up at Charlotte. She'd changed into a dark green bikini and held two dive masks and snorkels in her hands.

He tossed his phone aside. Smiling broadly, Jason sprang from his chair and caught up with Charlotte, the two running wild and laughing as their feet splashed into the surf.

THE END

JASON WAKE RETURNS

HOPE YOU ENJOYED this adventure. If you're looking to continue the escapades of Jason, Scott, Alejandra, and the rest of the team, you can stay up to date on new releases by signing up for my newsletter on my website:

MATTHEWRIEF.COM

Cheers to the next adventure,
Matthew

ACKNOWLEDGEMENTS

A SPECIAL THANKS TO the tribe of talented and brilliant individuals who strive to turn my sea story scribblings into something that's readable. First, I have the honor of working with Sarah Flores of Write Down the Line, a phenomenal editor who's literary improvement abilities never ceases to amaze me.

A big thank you to my two proofreaders, Donna Rich and Nancy Brown (Redline Proofreading). Their feedback and corrections are always helpful, and I can't say enough good things about them.

I'd also like to thank Stuart Bache from Books Covered for creating the outstanding cover for this book. And to Colleen Sheehan from Ampersand Book Interiors for adding the finishing touches with her fabulous designs and formatting.

Most importantly, I'd like to thank all of you incredible readers. It's an honor and dream to be able to write these adventures, and they wouldn't be possible without your support and recommendations of my stories.

ALSO BY MATTHEW RIEF

FLORIDA KEYS ADVENTURE SERIES:
Featuring Logan Dodge

Gold in the Keys
Hunted in the Keys
Revenge in the Keys
Betrayed in the Keys
Redemption in the Keys
Corruption in the Keys
Predator in the Keys
Legend in the Keys

Abducted in the Keys
Showdown in the Keys
Avenged in the Keys
Broken in the Keys
Payback in the Keys
Condemned in the Keys
Voyage in the Keys
Guardian in the Keys

JASON WAKE NOVELS

Caribbean Wake
Surging Wake
Relentless Wake

Turbulent Wake
Furious Wake
Perilous Wake

Join the Adventure!
Sign up for my newsletter to receive updates on upcoming books on my website:

MATTHEWRIEF.COM

ABOUT THE AUTHOR

MATTHEW HAS A deep-rooted love for adventure and the ocean. He loves traveling, diving, reading, and writing adventure novels. Though he grew up in the Pacific Northwest, he currently lives in Virginia Beach with his wife, Jenny.